CLIMATE FOR CONSPIRACY

We stopped talking abruptly. We had sensed rather than seen or heard something. We didn't move.

"What was that?" Melanie asked.

She was answered by three shots in rapid succession. Again we heard nothing but I saw flashes of light from the trees on our left. The first two bullets straddled us. The third threw up the snow at our feet—or that was my impression. We didn't stay to make sure.

Palma Harcourt

*Books by Palma Harcourt
from Jove*

A TURN OF TRAITORS
CLIMATE FOR CONSPIRACY

PALMA HARCOURT

CLIMATE FOR CONSPIRACY

A JOVE BOOK

This Jove book contains the complete
text of the original edition.
It has been completely reset in a typeface
designed for easy reading, and was printed
from new film.

CLIMATE FOR CONSPIRACY

A Jove Book/published by arrangement with
the author

PRINTING HISTORY
First published in Great Britain in 1974
by William Collins Sons & Co., Ltd.
Jove edition/May 1986

ISBN: 0-515-08511-1

Jove Books are published by The Berkley Publishing Group,
200 Madison Avenue, New York, N.Y. 10016.
The words "A JOVE BOOK" and the "J" with sunburst
are trademarks belonging to Jove Publications, Inc.

PRINTED IN THE UNITED STATES OF AMERICA

For Jack

PROLOGUE

I came out of the Foreign Office in a jubilant mood. I walked across the courtyard, under the archway and into Downing Street where, of course, there was a taxi. This was my lucky day.

Admittedly the taxi, painted a racing green, was a dilapidated old thing. It backfired harshly as it made a U-turn in front of the Chief Whip's office. The noise frightened into the air two pigeons which had been sunning themselves on the railing in front of Number 10 and disturbed the daydreams of the policeman on duty. He glared suspiciously, first at the cab and then, when I hailed it with an overexuberant wave of my briefcase, at me. I restrained a horrifying impulse, completely alien to me, to thumb my nose at him.

The taxi drew up beside me, backfiring yet again.

"Manchester Square—if you can make it."

The driver gave me a surly look. "I'll make it."

"Good. The quicker the better."

I was in a hurry now. The sooner the meeting with Dawson was over the sooner I could get home to Gaby and tell her the news. Tonight we would celebrate. My new posting wouldn't have been her first choice—she didn't like cold countries—but she would understand what it meant to me, that it was a plum of plums to which I hadn't dreamed of aspiring. For one thing I didn't have the seniority and for another, without being unduly modest, I didn't really have the experience. If I had thought about it at all I would have assumed that one of our more eminent ambassadors would be cross-posted or, if for some reason a career diplomat wasn't acceptable, that a big name would be chosen. But they had chosen me.

I, Mark Philip Lowrey, aged forty-two, was to be the first British Ambassador to the newly-created Republic of Canada. And, in addition, I was to be given my K! I hoped that Gaby would like being Lady Lowrey.

Hurriedly I wiped the self-satisfied smile from my face as the taxi turned into Manchester Square. In spite of its decrepitude, it had not only made it but it had made it in record time. I gave the driver a more than generous tip and watched him backfire down Spanish Place.

The tall blonde girl, who had opened the door to me, frowned at the noise and led me into a small office. From the Picasso print and the flowers on the desk, I judged it to be her own. She asked for my credentials. These she proceeded to check with meticulous care. I couldn't help asking myself what she would have done if they hadn't been in order—there didn't seem to be anyone else around—but I contained my impatience; it was always possible that she was a Black Belt. And, eventually, she gave them back to me.

"Mr. Dawson'll see you now," she said, "Room 1, first floor. There is a lift but the stairs are easier."

I raised an eyebrow but didn't comment. She hadn't offered to show me the way; she had opened a file and had at once become absorbed in it. I had been put in my place.

I walked up the broad, carpeted ·stairs and stood before Mr. Dawson's door. For a moment I hesitated. This was an odd establishment and I didn't know quite what to expect. Then I knocked sharply and was about to turn the handle when a voice said: "Enter."

The man who had spoken rose slowly from behind his desk. "Hello, Mark," he said. "Welcome to my lair. I imagine I must be something of a surprise to you."

As this was the understatement of the year I was pleased that my voice showed so little emotion. "Hello, Peregrine,"

I said. "I certainly never associated Mr. Dawson of Intelligence with the Honourable Peregrine Woods-Dawson."

"But it's not a name you'd forgotten. Even though it's a raft of years since we were at school together."

"I'd not forgotten it."

Woods-Dawson offered his hand across the desk. "I remember you too—very well. You were a clever small boy—and conscientious. I always thought you would go far." I sat in the chair to which he waved me and, to change the subject, said: "You were five years ahead of me, of course, but I heard that you'd got your double first at Oxford and passed high into the Foreign Office."

"Go on."

I shrugged. "I'm afraid I lost touch," I lied. I had heard plenty of gossip, some of it wild, especially as to what had caused his sudden disappearance from the diplomatic scene.

Woods-Dawson gave me a thin smile. "I know far more about you," he said, "far more. You've had what might be called a brilliant career in the Foreign Service, haven't you, Mark? And now your K—quite an achievement, considering how young you are."

"You know about the K too? You are well informed."

"Naturally. We must drink to further glory. What can I offer you?"

"Whisky and soda, please."

I swivelled my chair around and watched Woods-Dawson busy himself at a cabinet. Given the difference in his age, he hadn't changed unduly. He looked even more like a tall, thin version of the Duke of Wellington then he had at eighteen and there was the same sarcasm, the same sardonic sense of humour, the same force of character. I tried to ignore the feeling of uneasiness which he gave me; I no longer had to jump to the great man's commands and consider his whims. Deliberately I glanced at my wrist-watch.

"Too bad if you're in a hurry," he said. "We've a lot to discuss. But first let's drink to your success and mine."

Without commenting on the ambiguity of the toast I drank with him. The whisky was excellent, beautifully smooth. Obviously Woods-Dawson did himself well. I had already noted that his room was more like the library of a country house than a government office. I would like to have known his rank.

I said: "I've been very fortunate. There's a lot of luck in these things, as you know."

"And you're going to need all the luck you can get, dear boy."

For a second I was startled. Then I reassured myself; it had been such a typical Woods-Dawson remark. "I am?"

"You must realize what a hell of a posting you've been given."

"It should be—interesting."

"Interesting—to be the first British Ambassador to the new Republic of Canada! It's more likely to be bloody shattering, with an all-powerful President and a Prime Minister and a Parliament that don't really count. Surely you've been briefed on the political situation in that one-time bulwark of the Commonwealth, where you're going to represent Her Majesty?"

"Naturally," I said, determined not to be bullied by him.

Woods-Dawson shook his head in mock sadness. "And you think it'll be—interesting? God help us all."

I stifled my resentment—and my misgivings. I said: "I appreciate that Canada isn't a happy country. It's riven by too many different factions. And I know the President has taken a great deal of power. But, after all, it's only an adaptation of the French system, and the President seems to be doing rather well as a one-man show. There's not a vast amount of hostility towards Britain. In fact I believe there's a very good chance of replacing our old Commonwealth link by some sort of special relationship."

"Bully for you," Woods-Dawson said quietly.

It was a slap in the face. I took a deep breath—and expelled it slowly. I waited. There was nothing else to do. With deceptive mildness, Woods-Dawson continued.

"Mark, ever since the mid-sixties one of the top Russian projects has been to bring Canada into the Red sphere of influence. To achieve this they've done their utmost to isolate her from her Western Allies. At the moment they're cock-a-hoop because she's left the Commonwealth and their aim is to bring about a complete break with the UK. Any sort of special relationship between us is the last thing they want. And they'll go to any lengths and use any means to prevent it. They're not going to let some piddling little ambassador stand in their way. Do you understand that?"

"Yes, of course. I realize—"

"Well done!" He spoke as if I were his favourite pupil, who only needed a little encouragement to be quite bright. "Fortunately they're not going to be content with rendering you harmless. Had that been the case we could have saved them the trouble by sending some nonentity to Ottawa, which is precisely what the US has done. But no. They've picked His Excellency, Sir Mark Lowrey, for the part of victim."

I stared at him. "The part of victim? What in?"

"In the conspiracy to detach Canada from her remaining ties with the Western Alliance."

"But—" I said. "But—"

My incredulity seemed to infuriate Woods-Dawson. He thumped his glass on the desk and leaned towards me. "For Chrissakes! Believe me. I know." He bit off each word. "There is such a conspiracy and the British Ambassador— you, Mark—is going to be involved in it. Why else do you think you've been given such a prestigious post?"

I didn't want to believe him, God knows. My hopes had been so high and now . . . Feeling slightly sick, I said: "Are they planning to kidnap me, like James Cross and Pierre Laporte in 1970? Something like that?"

"I don't know what they're planning. I wish to hell I did." Woods-Dawson sounded grim. "But definitely not that. The last thing they want is to make a hero or a martyr out of you. No, you're to be the scapegoat, Mark. Somehow they're going to fix it so that you're sent home, with your tail between your legs—*persona non grata*—unless . . ." He shook his head.

"Unless?" I prompted.

"That we shall discuss, when you've stopped being starry-eyed about your posting."

I swallowed my bile. Of course Woods-Dawson was too astute not to have guessed how delighted I had been at the supposed plum which had been offered me, and too bloody-minded not to enjoy my present disillusionment. I decided to give him the minimum of satisfaction. I even managed a smile. I didn't realize that there was worse to come.

I said in my blandest manner: "I'm interested to know how you fit into the pattern, Peregrine."

"Dear Mark," he said. "Dear boy, I am to be your Nanny! And I shall arrange for you to have a nice red telephone, a scrambled line across the Atlantic, so that you'll be able to tell me all your secrets without anyone hearing anything they shouldn't."

It was after seven when I left the house in Manchester Square but time was no longer important; there was not—indeed there never had been—anything to celebrate. And I couldn't think what I was going to say to Gaby.

I had been with Woods-Dawson more than two hours and my ego was so deflated that I wasn't even angry, as I had every right to be.

Woods-Dawson had left me in no doubt as to why I, Mark Lowrey, was to be appointed British Ambassador to Canada. The Office had wanted somebody expendable who, when he made a mess of things—and the sods were pretty sure that he would make a mess of things—would cause, to quote Woods-Dawson, "only a little pooh and not a great nauseous stink" so that, as the political climate improved, they would be able to pick up the pieces and try again with someone else. But Woods-Dawson had considered such thinking a gross over-simplification and Woods-Dawson carried a lot of clout. He had maintained that if Britain in the person of her ambassador was discredited now it would be done in such a way that we would never have another opportunity to renew our ties with Canada; he had wanted an ambassador who, with Nanny's full support, would have a fighting chance to thwart the communists.

And they had compromised on me!

The tall blonde let me out of the house. She said: "Mr. Dawson's car is at your disposal, Mr. Lowrey. I've told Mrs. Lowrey that you're on your way. I telephoned earlier to let her know you'd be late."

I nodded. I didn't say thank you. I didn't feel grateful.

On the contrary I resented her proprietary tone; against my will I had acquired a nanny but I didn't need a nursemaid as well. However, there was no point in being petulant. I wished her good-night and was rewarded with a smile.

I sat back and let the chauffeur tuck an afghan around my legs. My mind reviewed what Peregrine Woods-Dawson had been telling me. The thought of having to work closely with him gave me no joy; still worse was the idea of working for him. At one point he had made it sound as if he intended to run me as an agent and I had threatened to refuse the posting. But he had been horrified and quick to placate me and he had said, with a sincerity that I couldn't question:

"Mark, you're not important. Neither am I. What is important is that the communists should fail and that Canada shouldn't be cut off from the Western Alliance. That is absolutely vital and it depends on us. God help us."

Thus passed my moment of rebellion. Now, for better or worse, I was committed—to Her Majesty, to be her representative in Ottawa, and to Woods-Dawson, to be heaven knows what. And once I had thought this was my lucky day!

PART ONE

Christmas

CHAPTER 1

December 16

NINE DAYS TO Christmas!

It was difficult to believe. I had been in Ottawa three whole months and some days. And I had accomplished damn all. I had met the President precisely once, when I presented my *lettres de créance*, and had seen little more of his Ministers, apart from the Trade chap who was very keen. So much for the special relationship I was hoping to forge between the UK and Canada.

Socially it was a different matter; Gaby and I had been inundated with invitations. And the public engagements too would have multiplied alarmingly if my old chum, Woods-Dawson, hadn't insisted on me cutting them to the bone. God knows what he thought this did for my image. I felt that I was becoming the prototype of the cocktail-swigging diplomat—except that I was very careful how much I drank.

I stared out of the bedroom window at the snow which lay deep on the garden of the Residence. I didn't believe Woods-Dawson was right to swaddle me as he was doing. Three whole months and no sign of a conspiracy; in fact not a bloody thing had happened. No one had tried to make me drunk so as to put me in some embarrassing position. No one had tried to commit suicide under the wheels of the ambassadorial car. No one had offered me his wife or his daughter or even his son for my enjoyment. No one had tried to do a damn thing. Britain and her Ambassador to

Canada remained beyond reproach.

But it had been three months of dull, nerve-grinding non-accomplishment. Thanks to Woods-Dawson, I had been fighting with shadows when there was a pile of real work to be done. I knew what my New Year's resolution was going to be. I had had enough of Woods-Dawson and his over-fertile imagination!

"A penny, darling." Gaby startled me.

I shook my head. "Not worth it."

"Please, Mark."

"All right. I was thinking that without Woods-Dawson's constant and blasphemous admonition to watch and pray I might have achieved more in the last few months."

"At least nothing ghastly has happened," she said. "When I think how terrified I was when we first came to Ottawa . . ." She left the sentence unfinished.

Abruptly I drew the curtains, shutting out the cold winter scene, and went across to her. She had been frightened for me, I knew, not for herself, and now she was trying to comfort me. Standing behind her, I put my hands on her narrow sloping shoulders and drew her to me. We smiled at our reflections in the mirror over her dressing-table. We were very close.

"Oh, darling!" I said. "I wish we could go to bed."

Her smile widened. "So do I, darling. But we can't."

"No." I heaved a sigh. "In fact, if you've finished painting your face, we had better go down and have a drink with that sister of mine before the rest of the party arrives."

"What an alternative!" Gaby laughed. "If only I had a choice." Then, suddenly serious, she turned to me. "Mark, try not to worry so much. At least try to relax and enjoy this evening. Please, darling."

"I'll do my best."

I kissed her on the tip of her long, well-bred nose and we went downstairs.

My sister, Melanie, was sipping a whisky and soda and reading the Ottawa newspaper. "Do you ever read the Letters in this rag of yours?" she asked, throwing the paper on the floor.

"Sometimes," I said.

"There's a disgusting one tonight."

Gaby picked up the paper and glanced at it. "You mean the one signed Canadian Patriot?"

"Yes. It infuriates me the way everyone's always prepared to throw stones at the States. Where does this Canadian Patriot think his country would be without her rich powerful neighbour?"

Gaby shrugged; she didn't want to argue with Melanie. "One can have too much—even of a good thing."

"I've a damn good mind to write to the paper myself."

"Oh no you don't!" I said. "Remember. No public speaking, no television appearances, no—letters to the editor. As long as you're in Canada you're the Ambassador's sister and a very private person."

"You mean Dr. Melanie Lowrey, the distinguished political scientist, had better button up her lip?"

"Quite. That's precisely what I do mean. Wait till you're back at Oxford."

"All right, dear brother. Until then I'll model myself on Gabrielle, serene and ornamental and—indifferent."

It was a direct gibe. Gaby winced but said nothing and I squirted soda viciously into my whisky so that it spilled over the tray, an excuse to swear, to relieve my feelings. Melanie had no right to be unkind to Gaby; her last remark was uncalled for and unjustified. Gaby was apolitical but certainly not apathetic. If Melanie was going to be bitchy I would regret inviting her to spend Christmas with us.

Come to think of it, we hadn't invited her. She had invited herself. She had telephoned unexpectedly from Washington where she had been at some academic get-together—I hadn't even known she was in the States—and asked if she might come for the rest of her vacation. I had been surprised because earlier she had written to say that she was going to Malta for Christmas with the history professor to whom she had been "engaged" for ten years or more. On the telephone she had been abrupt. Her plans had fallen through; could she come to us—or not? She had made it sound like an ultimatum.

Of course there had been no question, especially at Christmas. But when she arrived two days ago she was in

an odd mood, dispirited and on edge. Now she was being
bloody-minded. I sighed. There was enough to worry about,
what with Woods-Dawson glowering in the background
and—

That reminded me; I still hadn't told Woods-Dawson
Melanie was in Ottawa. In the event I had had neither time
nor inclination to consult him. Indeed the very idea of asking
his permission to invite my own sister to stay riled me.
Nevertheless it would be a courteous gesture to mention it
during our next transatlantic conversation. There was no
point in making Nanny angry over an unimportant issue.

Gaby was telling Melanie about the guests whom we
were expecting for dinner.

"So that I don't put an undiplomatic foot in it," Melanie
said.

"Then there are Alex and Sally Stocker," Gaby said. "You
met the Stockers at our house a couple of years ago, before
they were posted out here."

"I remember." Melanie sniffed. "A harassed little man
with a very sexy wife, considerably younger than himself."

"You don't flatter my Minister," I said drily.

"Do I exaggerate?" Melanie shrugged. "He was Acting
Head of Mission in Ottawa before you arrived, wasn't he?
It must have been a blow to him when you were made
Ambassador. Does he hate your guts for it, Mark?"

"No," I said, "I don't think so. Anyway there was never
any question of him being H.E."

"Does he know that?" Gaby asked.

"I've no idea." I glanced at my watch. "Tell her about
the others, darling. They'll be arriving in a minute."

I got up and leaned against the mantel, kicking irritably
at a log which was threatening to fall out of the fire, while
Gaby continued with her thumbnail sketches. She was rather
good at them.

"Edgar King!" Melanie said. "Of course. He used to be
a great friend of Mark's when they were up at Oxford."

"He still is a great friend," I said firmly, though, to be
truthful, our relationship wasn't as easy as it had been.

Melanie ignored my comment. "I think Mark was rather
proud of knowing a Rhodes Scholar from Canada. And

Father was very fond of him. So he was always coming to stay with us. But that was years ago—before he was married. What's his wife like?"

"Heather," Gaby said, answering the question obliquely, "only likes successful people. She considers you one."

Melanie laughed. "How nice! I look forward to meeting her. And who's the odd man? I'm up to thirteen, including us, and I'm sure you won't have left it at that."

"Walter Eland," I said, "who used to be a great friend of yours when he was at Canada House, London."

And that was something of an understatement. Gaby and I had both been convinced that Melanie would marry Walter. (At the time she was having a row with her history professor over one of his more seductive pupils and their affaire was in abeyance.) We were sorry when nothing came of it. Originally Edgar had written to introduce Walter as some sort of cousin as well as close friend and colleague in External Affairs but we had soon become attached to him for his own sake. I would have liked him for a brother-in-law: I couldn't stand the Oxford chap.

"Walter Eland!" Gaby repeated when Melanie said nothing. "Don't pretend you've forgotten him, Melanie. He'll be terribly hurt if you do."

"I wouldn't dream of being so childish," Melanie said. She finished her whisky and put down the glass with a thud. "Anyway no one could forget a man who had such a resemblance to a thin sad walrus!" she added bitterly.

In the doubtful silence that followed we heard the front-door bell. And our guests began to arrive.

The party got going very quickly. It was small enough and informal enough and people were sufficiently acquainted for it to make itself. No effort was required from Gaby or me. I looked forward to a happy, relaxing evening and thought how much this would please her.

I hoped Melanie would enjoy it too; everyone was going out of their way to be pleasant to her, talking about her books and her lectures and her television appearances. I always forget that my sister's something of a celebrity, at any rate in England, and Walter, I suspect, had been blowing an advance trumpet for her here. He had certainly seemed delighted to see her again and grateful for a peck on the cheek.

I was unprepared when Alex Stocker got me to one side. "Mark, can I have a word with you? Something's come up."

"Must you?" I wasn't pleased.

Alex shrugged. "You left early tonight. There was a telephone call after you'd gone."

"Wait a minute."

I hadn't meant to sound quite so abrupt. But I had just poured Gaby some sherry and I didn't see why she should have to wait. Alex couldn't have anything urgent to tell me or he would have got in touch before. Besides I resented the implication that I ought to have been at the Chancery; I hadn't imagined a reproof—or had I? Most likely it was just Alex fussing about formalities. He had probably dealt with the matter himself, whatever it was, but wanted me to be aware of the fact. I decided to give him the benefit of the doubt.

I took the sherry across to Gaby. The women, except for Sally Stocker, who had cornered our most attractive male guest, seemed to have gathered in a group in front of the fire. Heather King was dominating the conversation, telling Melanie all the things she must see and do before she went back to England. I grinned. My sister was going to be busy; she would soon be exhausted before the Hilary term began.

I lingered with them briefly, then went back to Alex.

To placate him I said: "Sorry to dash away like that. You were saying—a telephone call?"

"Yes. It was a man's voice, obviously disguised. He spoke English with a French accent but that could have been put on too. He needn't have been a Franco. I don't think he was."

I frowned. I dislike the division of Canadians into Francos and Anglos according to their first language. "I assume he gave no name. What did he want?"

"To speak to you. He was very insistent. No one but the Ambassador would do. Eventually he settled for me when I swore to deliver his message but he didn't like it. If you had been there . . . He didn't sound like the usual crank. He wasn't threatening or abusive or downright bonkers, just very earnest. I got the impression that he really believed what he said and he wanted you to know."

"Know what, Alex?"

"Oh, sorry. Am I being long-winded? Well, he wanted to warn you, he said. There's some sort of a plot and you may be in danger." Alex had lowered his voice so that I had to lean towards him to hear what he was saying. "He said you have enemies. Some of them are supposedly old friends. But you should trust nobody. Nobody."

"Was that all?"

"More or less. He banged down the receiver—nearly broke my ear-drum—as if he'd been interrupted or had had second thoughts about what he was doing." Alex stopped. Some of my tension must have communicated itself to him. He said quickly: "Mark, I shouldn't worry. I could have been wrong. I expect he was another odd-ball."

I grinned at him reassuringly. He meant to be kind. Besides, I didn't want him to know that I might take such a warning seriously. He knew nothing about the threat of a communist conspiracy; Woods-Dawson had been adamant that he shouldn't be told. "Probably," I agreed. "Anyway I'll be able to judge for myself in the morning."

"Judge for yourself?"

"You had the call taped, didn't you? There was plenty of opportunity."

"Yes, but—I—didn't think of it. I'm sorry."

"You mean we have no record of the damn thing?"

"No," Alex said miserably, an ugly flush spreading up his neck as he glowered into his whisky.

He was twelve years my senior and I had once worked under him. I bit my tongue. "That's—disappointing," I said, thinking of some of the stronger words which Woods-Dawson would apply to the situation. "However, there's nothing we can do about it. Let's go and join the others, shall we?" There was no need to add that future calls, if any, should be taped.

"Yes," Alex said, and followed me meekly.

I attached myself to the larger group of our guests and

Alex had the tact to drift away to the smaller. The conversation was concerned with the masked ball to be held at the National Arts Centre the following night. Everyone seemed to be going—except Gaby and me.

The French Ambassador had bidden us to dine with him, a diplomatic invitation which couldn't be refused. To be honest, we were glad of it. Although we both love dancing we hate fancy-dress affairs. It's a phobia which seems to run in the Lowrey family. It's certainly shared by Melanie. Having agreed to partner Walter to the Ball, she was horrified to discover she was expected to play Alice to his White Rabbit. She was expostulating loudly when the bomb went off.

At the time we didn't know it was a bomb.

There was a muffled booming sound outside the house. The window of the drawing-room shattered. A heavy object fell on to the carpet; only the double-glazing and the weight of the velvet curtains prevented it from flying into the room and doing God knows what damage. The curtains billowed and subsided. A blast of Arctic air rushed in upon us. There was a suspended hush.

Then one of the women screamed.

A man shouted: "Take cover!"

The houseman, who had been butling for us, reacted immediately; he switched off the lights and ran to the window, pausing only for the briefest glance at the object on the floor before he drew back the curtains. Everyone else dived behind the bits of furniture, including me. My first reaction had been to pull Gaby down behind the sofa; once she was safe I was prepared to be brave. There was general confusion. Someone knocked over a table and glass broke.

The front door banged. Running footsteps echoed down the driveway. I was on my feet in time to see the burly back of my chauffeur in the black sweater and pants which he wears as an off-duty uniform making for the road.

I stared out of the broken window and shivered at the cold. There was nothing to be seen except the snow, dazzling in the moonlight, the long shadows cast by the trees and the bulk of cars belonging to my guests. The house opposite was in darkness.

For years a succession of British representatives to Canada lived at Earnscliffe, a beautiful old stone house which had once belonged to the Father of Confederation, Sir John A. Macdonald. However, after the last High Commissioner moved out, the place was burnt down by some anti-British elements who had been unaware that it was to be a gift from Britain to the people of Canada; and, as had always been intended, the Residence of the first British Ambassador was in Rockcliffe Park, a posh suburb of Ottawa. Here our neighbours were other diplomats, senior government servants, high-ranking service officers and a fair sample of rich business people. None of these seemed to be taking the least notice of the disturbance. Somehow I found this reassuring; the danger, whatever it had been, was past.

As if to confirm my view, the houseman said: "It's all right, Sir Mark." He was on his knees, examining the object which had been blasted through the window. "Just our bad luck it blew in here. Look!"

I bent down and looked. He was pointing at some lettering on what appeared to be a piece of metal. I read it: IL—COURRIER. Half of the English word "MAIL" had gone but the French was intact. And at once I knew what had happened. Someone had planted a bomb in the post-box at the end of our drive and blown the thing to bits. It was, as he had said, just luck that a chunk had come through the window of the British Residence. Our bad luck—or someone's good luck? There had been that telephone warning which might or might not be relevant.

But this was no time for philosophizing.

People were moving behind me. Alex was already leaning over my shoulder to inspect the object and muttering at me. Walter had gone to the window. I remembered that there was broken glass on the carpet where a table had been overturned; I didn't want an accident, somebody getting badly cut and needing medical attention. The less publicity the better. The murmur of voices, enquiring, frightened, one rather upset, another angry, was growing.

The houseman said: "May I suggest, sir? A drink in your study—I'll bring in a tray—and dinner in twenty minutes."

I nodded. "Can you board the window?"

"Yes."

"Good. Put on the lights. I'll draw the curtains."

"Yes, Sir Mark."

The houseman spoke in a loud voice, deferentially, as if I had been issuing orders to him right and left when, in fact, he had been more in control of the situation than anyone. But then he was an excellent servant, with unusual qualities; so were the chauffeur and the cook. Each of them had been hand-picked by Woods-Dawson from some domestic agency which never advertised in *The Times*.

"Please stay where you are for a moment, everyone," I said, "until we can get some light."

The velvet curtains thudded gently together, shutting out the moonlight, the snow and most of the Arctic air. I caught a glimpse of my chauffeur loping back to the house. And the room was flooded with light again.

The scene was slightly shocking. Our elegant party had disintegrated. Not only was there glass and liquor staining the carpet but the table itself had been broken; the portly guest, who must have fallen heavily upon it, was still sitting on the floor. Someone else had knocked over an azalea. The pot was intact but the plant broken, earth and rose-coloured petals scattered over a chair. Everyone seemed more or less embarrassed.

"I do apologize for all the excitement," Gaby said in her clear, cool voice, easing the tension. "I only hope it hasn't upset Cook. That would be a real calamity. She's a superb *cuisinière* but temperamental as one might expect."

I caught the eye of the houseman whose unflappable wife Gaby had just maligned and hurriedly looked away. I said, as my sister opened her mouth to make some cutting comment on what she would consider Gaby's failure to get her priorities right: "I suggest we go along to my study. Then we can have the drink which we must all need to calm our nerves. I think the post-box outside has been blown up. But there isn't another anywhere near so we're quite safe from any more flying objects and fortunately this one hasn't done much damage. Will you lead the way, Gaby?"

The crisis over, conversation burst out amid laughter and
small acts of self-assurance. Bombs in mail-boxes were no
new things to Ottawans, though they had had none for over
a year. Now there were stories to be told, incidents to be
remembered. My guests allowed themselves to be shep-
herded from the room without any fuss. Walter was a great
help.

Only Edgar remained, leaning against the wall; he looked
ill. Normally he had the high colour which often goes with
sandy hair but now his face was putty-pale and his skin had
a greenish tinge. In one hand he held a tumbler, a quarter
full of neat whisky, to which he had helped himself. I wondered how much he had already drunk.

"Come on, Edgar," I said. "Let's join the rest of them.
Then the room can be cleared up. There's quite a mess,
isn't there?"

He stared at me. He had small, very blue eyes. He began
to say something, stuttered and took a swig of whisky. I
had never seen him in such a state before. Why, for heaven's
sake?

I was trying to word a tactful question when he thrust
his glass at me and ran. Luckily he managed to contain
himself until he reached the cloakroom. I followed him into
the hall. From there I could hear him vomiting into the
lavatory pan. He hadn't had time to shut the door so I shut
it for him, very gently. I doubt that he noticed.

I turned to find my chauffeur. He was almost as pale as
Edgar had been but his voice was level.

"It was the post-box, sir. A heavy charge for the job.
Debris's scattered all over the place."

"Much damage?"

He shook his head. "Apart from the fluke piece through
our window and a gash on one of the cars. Mr. King's
Chrysler."

"Oh, dear!" I said. "Mrs. King will not be pleased." In
fact she would be furious, though it was an old car; Edgar
was hanging on to it in expectation of a posting in the spring.
"Anything else before I call the police? I can't leave it too
long in case someone else makes a report."

"Thomas, sir," he said and suddenly swore violently. "He must've been out for his evening walk when the thing went off. He caught the blast. He's plastered over the elm tree. It's a horrid mess."

"Hell!" I said, understanding my chauffeur's pallor.

Thomas was a cat, a black tom. He had turned up on our doorstep, an obvious stray, soon after we arrived in Ottawa and had become very sleek from Cook's spoiling. He was part of the family—our luck, perhaps. His death would make the whole household miserable. Poor old Thomas!

But the frightening thing was that it could as easily have been one of us or one of our guests, and the big question which Woods-Dawson would want answered was whether or not it was chance that this particular post-box so close to the British Residence had been chosen.

Full of misgivings, I went to telephone the Canadian Federal Police.

CHAPTER 2

December 18

"AND NOW THE weather for Ottawa and the Valley. Clear, with some cloudy periods and a few scattered flurries later in the day. Very cold. Winds 15, gusting to 20. High today, 5 above. Expected low tonight, 10 below. Present temperature at the Château, 7 below. Humidity, 47 per cent. With the windchill factor it all adds up this December morning to a brisk 35 degrees below zero.

"And to re-cap, here are the news headlines: The Canadian Federal Police have arrested a suspect in the mailbox bombings. At the request of the US and UK Ambassadors, guards on their Residences will be withdrawn some forty-odd hours after the bombings. The Prime Minister has recovered from influenza and is returning to the House. The Minister of Agriculture has announced that the sale of wheat . . ."

The announcer's voice sighed to a halt as I turned off the car radio: I didn't want to listen to any more. I leaned back in the comfort of the Rolls—I was on my way downtown to the Chancery—and looked through the window at the shining day with its sun bright in a deep blue sky. The brightness was deceptive. It was bitterly cold, the sort of bone-chilling cold that people who have always lived in temperate climates can't even imagine. In such weather there was no joy for the CFP keeping a round-the-clock watch on the Residence and anyway they served no purpose; the danger was over. And I would be as glad to be rid of them as doubtless they would be glad to leave. A police guard was the worst publicity.

Woods-Dawson had stressed that point. He was in an acid mood. Somehow he had got hold of the idea that the Americans had dealt with their bomb incident more diplomatically than I had. I argued that they had merely been luckier. The Ambassador and his family had been out for the evening, the servants at the back of the house had been watching television, and the passer-by who had found the debris of the post-box while walking his dog had telephoned the police from his own house. The Americans had thus been able to adopt a detached attitude to the whole thing.

I hadn't been so fortunate. Splendid aloofness had scarcely been possible. Everything was against it: I had been giving a dinner-party for my well-known sister—Woods-Dawson, quite unnecessarily, damn him, had breathed flames over our transatlantic line when he learned that Melanie, whom he described as "that pro-American hawk," was spending Christmas with us; my guests had been questioned by the CFP; a piece of metal had gone through my drawing-room window; my chauffeur had been the first to inspect the remains of the post-box; a car that was damaged belonged to one of my guests—Heather, as expected, had made the most stupid fuss over the Kings' old Chrysler; even the poor cat which had been blown to pieces was mine and so British by adoption. But Woods-Dawson wasn't interested in excuses: I was to damp down the whole affair as much as possible.

He didn't say how but he did say why. He was convinced that this was the beginning of the long-awaited communist campaign against me.

As far as I could see, however, we were still at square one, watching and praying, and likely to stay there. I didn't believe that the police would get anything worthwhile out of the unfortunate suspect whom they had arrested—I was to be proved right about that, at any rate—and the telephone warning which had preceded the bombing was no help. I had made Alex Stocker write down the message as he re-

membered it but he had a lousy memory and nothing had
been achieved, except that he had been irritated.

Woods-Dawson was more than irritated. He insisted that
I should take my finger out and report to him at once if
anything in the least untoward happened. I hadn't done too
well over the post-box bomb, it seemed, so Nanny was
going to tie me to a tighter apron-string.

I sighed. We were almost at the Chancery. I had intended
to have a sandwich at my desk today and make up some
paper work before the importance of the afternoon but suddenly I couldn't face it. I opened the glass panel which
separated me from the chauffeur and said:

"I'm going home to lunch. Twelve forty-five."

"Very good, Sir Mark."

The beautifully-kept Rolls with its Union Jack fluttering
drew up in front of the Chancery entrance. The chauffeur
opened the car door and stood to attention, his breath bal-
looning into the frozen air, while I made a dignified dash
into the building. Even in that short distance the Arctic wind
sliced through me and I was thankful to get inside.

Yet, perversely, I found my office oppressive, hot and
airless. I set the thermostat ten degrees lower and got down
to work. Nothing much had come in from London during
the night so I whistled through the telegrams and started on
the post. I wrote "Accept" on invitations to speak in the
New Year to the Canadian Institute of International Affairs
and the Canadian Club. The dates didn't clash with my
proposed visit to the Arctic and Woods-Dawson would ap-
prove, I hoped. The University of Ottawa he would probably
turn down; he distrusted all students. And the Ottawa Chap-
ter of the Imperial Order of the Daughters of the Empire I
didn't need to consult him about; "Refuse" I wrote firmly,
grinning.

On a more social level Sir Mark and Lady Lowrey were
invited to three receptions, two dinner-parties and a luncheon. I skimmed through these. The invitation to the skating party I kept until last.

As was her practice, my secretary had put a neat little
tick in the upper right-hand corner to show that I hadn't a
previous engagement, but whatever she had put wouldn't

have made any difference. There was no question of refusal. This was a royal command.

On New Year's Day Gaby and I—and Melanie, which showed how efficiently the Presidential staff kept tabs on one—were invited to enjoy skating and a champagne supper at Rideau Palace. Dress was to be informal.

For a minute I fingered the gold coat of arms embossed on the card and pictured all the diplomats and their ladies in formal skating garb. For some reason I saw it as a Victorian scene, bustles, tail-coats, tiaras, and resplendent orders—myself chatting with the President. What a hope! I was smiling broadly when the Minister came in.

"Good morning, Mark."

"Morning, Alex."

"You're very cheerful?"

"Not really. But there's a certain amount of quiet fun to be had from my correspondence."

"Well, you don't read the hate mail."

"True. I gather it's increasing in bulk during this charitable season."

Alex nodded, smothering a yawn. "Sorry," he apologized. "We were at the Arts Centre Ball last night. Sally insisted on staying till the end and I can't stand missing my sleep as I used to."

"I don't imagine you're the only one somewhat the worse for wear this morning. But you enjoyed it, I hope? Melanie said it was a splendid affair."

"Yes, it was. Pity you had to miss it."

"Yes."

Our small talk over we got down to some bits of business, the advisability of having a British Week in the major University towns across Canada, the minimum of entertainment due to a party of our left-wing parliamentarians on their way to or from an international peace rally in Toronto, and one or two minor problems on the domestic front.

"Anything else?" I asked, wondering how best to broach the subject of Sally Stocker's debts, which was yet another domestic problem, so far unmentioned.

"Yes, there is something," Alex said. He fidgeted in his

chair as if he were uncomfortable. "It's about that telephone warning you had, before the bomb went off in your post-box."

"Yes," I said. "What about it?" I was surprised that he had again brought up what to him was a sore subject.

"I've been thinking about it," he said. "Not—not deliberately, you understand—that didn't get me anywhere—but it's been at the back of my mind. And I've remembered—the trouble is, Mark, I'm not really sure. Perhaps I shouldn't have mentioned it."

"For God's sake, you haven't mentioned anything yet." I curbed my impatience. "Alex, what do you think you remember?"

"He said—the man who telephoned, when he was warning you not to trust anyone, not even your old friends—he said something about distrusting new friends too, or perhaps it was that you oughtn't to make any new friends. I—I'm sorry. Hell! I wish I'd had the damn thing taped."

I very nearly said something honest and unforgivable but instead I thanked him for telling me about it. "Not to worry," I said blithely. "It's not really important."

Alex nodded his agreement and began to collect his papers together. "Incidentally," he said, "good luck for this afternoon."

"Thanks. I shall probably need it."

"I always hate press conferences myself." He had all his papers by now and was standing up. "The best of British luck," he said and laughed at his own joke.

I opened my mouth to bring up the unpleasant subject of Sally's debts and shut it again. I let him walk out of the room. My courage had failed me. Now I would have to write him a personal memo because something had to be done; we couldn't have irate dress-shops dunning the Chancery for their money. Damn Sally Stocker! Why couldn't she pay her bills? Why did she have to be the one? . . . I swore gently. Ah well, perhaps a memo would be less embarrassing all around.

By two o'clock I was back at my desk studying the news-

papers and priming myself for the big event of the day, my
first press conference in Canada.

This was extremely important or it could be, not least
because it was to be shown later on the CBC television
network at prime time, usurping God knows what favourite
programme. I was praying that I wouldn't make a mess of
things. I was also doing my homework; I wanted to muff
as few questions as possible.

Because of the bomb episode Woods-Dawson, who had
never been exactly keen, had wanted to cancel the conference but for once, after a long argument, I had won. I had
persuaded him that a sudden cancellation would antagonize
the press, who had been quite kind to me up to now. I didn't
tell him that I looked upon this conference as a possible
turning-point. It was, after all, the perfect forum from which
to begin to foster the new relationship between Britain and
Canada and we had to begin somewhere. I was tired of
inactivity.

Of course there were inherent dangers. Better men than
I had been made to appear fools or knaves when questioned
by the press but nothing wager, nothing gain. Reluctantly
Woods-Dawson had agreed—after I had sworn to see a
threat in every question and a double meaning in the simplest
remark. He had imbued me with his nervousness if nothing
else.

I rifled through the pages of the *Globe and Mail* restlessly.
And a small paragraph, tucked away in an insignificant
corner, caught my eye. I read it with interest. The Department of External Affairs had announced some postings. Two
ambassadors were swapping missions early in the New Year
and the third, one of their senior men, was coming home
in the spring. It was not known who would take his place
but "the name of Mr. Walter Eland has been mentioned."

I knew what that meant. Someone's face would be very
red if Walter didn't get the Brussels job now. I would have
to ring him up and congratulate him. It was a plum. Iron-
ically it was one of the plums for which Edgar had been
hoping. Well, he wouldn't begrudge it to Walter; he was
always generous. Heather was the one who would bitch.

Poor old Edgar! Nothing seemed to be going right for him at the moment.

I got up from my desk and stretched. The room was chilly—my own fault because I had forgotten to reset the thermostat. I turned it up a few degrees, then strolled over to the window and looked out at the cold, bleak, grey-white landscape below. I was wondering how different Canada's history might have been if Queen Victoria, sticking her apocryphal pin in the map, had picked Toronto or Montreal as the nation's capital when my Press Secretary came in. It was time to get down to work again.

For the next hour he briefed me on the people I was about to meet and the problems they might present me with. He did it very well and with great thoroughness. I got the impression that he was determined that, if I did make a mess of things, nobody would be able to say it was his fault; but maybe I was being oversensitive. Anyway I did my best to be a receptive pupil.

At ten past three we left for the Press Building and my first North American press conference.

A formal press conference is always something of an effort. Newsmen, on the whole, are intelligent and tenacious; they are also able to research their questions in advance. The unfortunate character in the hot seat has to be prepared to leap from one subject to the next and, however well he may be briefed and however good his memory, he can't be an expert on every related matter. Moreover, apart from answers which he doesn't know, there are answers which he doesn't want to give and yet others which he ought not to give because the follow-up will devastate him—all this from a seemingly friendly audience, amongst whom there often lurks a real sod.

And constantly, at the back of my mind must be Woods-Dawson's admonitions. It was no wonder I was tense.

Fortunately, however, thanks to the doyen of the Press Corps, a most charming and easy man, who was waiting to greet me, a good deal of my nervousness had dissipated by the time he and I walked on to the platform. He sat me beside him and, while he made some brief, complimentary remarks by way of introduction, I looked at the rows of faces in front of me; the small theatre was packed. I noticed one or two people made familiar by television and then the questions began.

"The opening questions were what I had expected. They came from newsmen many of whose names were known to me from their columns or from television and radio. They gave me an excellent chance, without sounding too pompous, to expound on Britain's desire for a relationship with Canada based on old friendship and new respect. I was grateful for them.

They were followed by questions on the strict British immigration laws, which led to the subjects of race, foreign aid, trade—especially trade with Canada. At this point I was confounded by the *Financial Post* man, who dazzled me and, I suspect, everyone else, by a pyrotechnic display of statistics. I did the only thing I could, admitted that I didn't have a clue but added that if he would telephone the Chancery the next day my expert would give him all the answers. It was an amicable interchange.

Then came the inevitable query about the "mail-box bombs" and I was involved in violence, Quebec separatism and the two-nations theory. I had said before the conference began that I didn't want an interpreter—I speak French fluently, though by no means as perfectly as Gaby—and any question addressed to me in French I answered in that language. Such an unexpected talent on the part of the British Ambassador produced a compliment from *Le Droit* and a burst of half-ironic applause from the rest of the audience.

Taking advantage of the lightness of the atmosphere and perhaps to give me a brief respite, the chairman nodded at an attractive red-head. I didn't catch the name of her paper but she looked as if she wrote a social column or was the editor of a woman's magazine. In a little girl's voice she asked if it was my policy not to attend public functions in Ottawa such as the National Arts Centre Ball. It seemed the silliest question.

"Of course not," I said. "My wife and I regretted having to miss the Ball but we had a long-standing engagement to

dine with the French Ambassador. However," I added gra-
tuitiously, "my sister, who's spending Christmas with us,
went and enjoyed it very much."

"I know," the red-headed girl said. "Your sister, Dr. Melanie Lowrey, has just come up from Washington, hasn't
she? She was conferring on a matter of importance with
government officials there. Can you tell me, Sir Mark, is
Dr. Lowrey a very close friend of Mr. John Coller's?"

I was completely thrown. The name of John Coller was
dimly familiar but not in association with Melanie. Somehow I connected it with my Press Secretary but I couldn't
remember how. It seemed to me that in a lengthening silence
I gaped and groped and fumbled. Later, when I watched
the replay on television I was pleasurably surprised to see
that I hadn't carried it off too badly.

"My sister was at an academic conference in Washington," I corrected her, after only the slightest of hesitations.
"As for Mr. Coller, I wouldn't know whether or not he was
one of her many friends and acquaintances."

"Thank you very much, Your Excellency," the red-head
said with a wide smile, and sat down.

I turned with relief to the next inquisitor. He wanted to
know about the Carmine Project, a subject on which I was
well briefed and enthusiastic. So evidently was the Press
Corps. Questions snowballed.

Yes, six stations were planned. So far none had been
completed.

No, I hadn't visited the Arctic yet. I hoped to go in the
New Year.

It was possible but not probable that cities would grow
up around these research stations. The cost of building on
the permafrost was prohibitive.

Yes, the Russians had done it in their North. Maybe
Canada would do the same sometime. But that was no
concern of the Carmine Project. As its full name, the Canadian Arctic Mineral Exploration Project implied, the purpose of Carmine was to explore the whole of the potential
mineral resources in the Canadian Arctic.

Certainly Canada had retained her mineral rights.

Yes, the Project was British in the sense that the idea

had originated in the UK and the British Government had put up much of the capital. But Anglo-Canadian would be a better word. The Canadian Government was co-operating fully.

I was on delicate ground; there was a lot of politics involved. Out of the corner of my eye I saw the chairman looking at his watch and hoped I would be saved by the bell. I answered a couple more questions and then somebody asked me in bad French how much American money had gone into Carmine.

"None at all," I said. "The Americans have no sort of interest in the Project."

To my surprise and annoyance he then repeated the question in English and, very politely, requested that I should give the same answer in that language, which I did. I had no choice. But I objected to his manner.

Almost immediately the conference came to an end and we adjourned for drinks and sandwiches. I made my excuses as soon as possible.

It was now my turn, as we were driven back to the Chancery, to ask questions. The answers weren't very satisfactory.

My Press Secretary didn't know the man who had demanded a bi-lingual statement about Carmine but believed he was connected with one of the university newspapers. He had never seen the red-haired girl before and knew nothing of her; without meaning to, he managed to imply that surely she and her questions were unimportant. And when I mentioned John Coller, he roared with laughter.

"Of course I know John," he said. "He's my opposite number. He's in charge of Press and Public Relations at the US Embassy." He stopped abruptly. "I'm afraid I don't understand, sir. You say you've never heard of John Coller but he took your sister to the Arts Centre Ball last night."

I stared at him in amazement. "He did not!" I said. "She went with Walter Eland—who's an old friend of mine in External Affairs."

Without speaking, he took the newspaper, which was folded under his arm, turned to an inner page and passed it to me. It was a copy of the local rag, and it had gone to town on the Ball; there was a double spread of photographs in colour with appropriate captions. I recognized Melanie and Walter at once. Melanie, as Alice, was wearing a narrow blue mask which did nothing to disguise her; Walter, on the other hand, was invisible in his White Rabbit suit. The caption read: "Dr. Melanie Lowrey, sister of the British Ambassador, with Mr. John Coller of Washington, a close friend."

"I see," I said with relief. "That explains a lot. The paper has got the name wrong. Melanie's partner was Walter Eland, who *is* a close friend. I don't suppose she has ever met John Coller."

He grinned. "Ah well," he said, "that's the way rumours start—especially with a gay bachelor like John."

"Yes, indeed," I said absently; I should have paid more attention but my mind was running through the press conference again. On the whole, I decided, it had been a success. I had been lucky and I had done pretty well. Woods-Dawson should be pleased. So why, why, I asked myself, did I have this queasy feeling in the pit of my stomach? I told myself it was just reaction.

CHAPTER 3

December 19, morning

AS I LINGERED over breakfast, the telephone rang. Heather King wanted to speak to Gaby. Relieved that the call wasn't for me, I poured myself another cup of coffee and drank it slowly, my back half turned to the window so that I shouldn't see the Rolls waiting to take me to the Chancery. I was going to be late in this morning but I didn't care. I was feeling lazy.

Melanie said: "Mark, you'll never guess what Gaby and I are doing today."

"What?"

"Sight-seeing."

"You can't be serious."

"I am. We're visiting the Parliament Buildings and the Centennial Flame and the National Library and God knows what else."

I laughed. "Who's organizing this? Not Gaby?"

"Not me, darling," Gaby said, coming back into the room. "Heather. She has been planning an orgy of *tourisme* for Melanie. But, alas, her plans have gone awry."

"Good," Melanie said.

"We're leaving in half an hour," Gaby warned her. "But Heather's abandoning us at *The Canada Goose* at twelve. Could you possibly pick us up there, Mark? Incidentally, I forgot to tell you, they telephoned yesterday to say that they

34

had a new consignment from Cape Dorset and there were some prints amongst it."

"Then I'll certainly pick you up." Opened by the Department of Northern Affairs as an outlet for Eskimo and Indian work, *The Canada Goose* is my favourite shop and I'm always ready to visit it. "But why's Heather letting you off so easily?"

"Because Edgar told her—when they were getting ready for bed last night—that he proposed to bring some VIP home for lunch today. She has been up since five preparing a gourmet meal. She was furious."

"If he were my husband I'd tell him to go to hell," Melanie said. "Why doesn't she?"

"She wouldn't turn down a VIP," I said uncharitably. "It might hurt Edgar's career and that she'd never do. She's going to make him an Under-Secretary before he retires or kill him in the attempt."

"Edgar has also commanded a snowmobiling party for the weekend," Gaby said. "Heather suggested Sunday, but—"

"Not Sunday," I said.

"Darling, I know," Gaby murmured.

I said to Melanie: "It was my first rule when I became a Head of Mission. Sunday is a private day, for family only, unless the enemy are actually battering down the Chancery doors—which reminds me. If I don't appear soon Alex'll be telephoning to see if His Excellency is indisposed. I must fly."

Gaby said: "Mark, not Sunday. Melanie's going ski-ing with the Stockers anyhow. But I promised Saturday. It was difficult to refuse and it might be fun, I suppose, if it's not too cold. Is that all right?"

"Of course, darling."

Gaby followed me into the hall. "I'm afraid it may be a very organized party," she said. "Heather hinted that Edgar wants you to meet someone who's on the President's personal staff."

"M-mm," I said. I was interested. "Did she mention his name?"

"No, but he's some relation of Edgar's. I'll ask about

him during our sight-seeing."

"Fine." There was no need to tell Gaby to make her enquiries tactfully. I bent and kissed her. "Goodbye, darling. Have a good time and don't let Heather make you plough around in the snow too much."

"I won't," she promised. "Bye, Mark. And don't forget—after twelve at *The Canada Goose.*"

At five past twelve, in good time to meet Gaby and Melanie in the Northern Affairs shop, I left the car at the intersection of Sparks Street and Metcalfe Street and began to walk along the Mall. It was, I thought, no day for sight-seeing.

Ottawa was not at its best. The leaden sky cast a gloom over the cold grey buildings; the suddenly soaring temperature was turning the snow to muddy slush under foot and blocked drains formed stagnant pools of dirty water; the Christmas decorations were bedraggled and pathetic; and from the papermills across the river there came the revolting smell of sulphite, shaming to a rich capital. I felt rather sorry for Heather and hoped that Melanie hadn't been too caustic.

I passed a couple of Canadian Federal Police, skirted a huge piece of out-door sculpture and reached *The Canada Goose.* The heavy, pneumatic door sighed shut behind me and I was in a different world.

Sealskin gloves, moccasins, bags with leather fringe, beads and brooches of painted wood, carvings made from walrus tusks, parkas fashioned from Hudson Bay blankets, driftwood sculpture, masks, textiles, a birchbark canoe, all crowded floor and tables and hung on walls. The first impression was one of colour, subtle browns and greys with great splashes of primaries. The next was that everything, even the most insignificant object, had been made with loving care because hands and tools had been used, not machines. It was a delightful place.

I stood just inside the entrance and looked around. Lunchtime, the week before Christmas, meant that the shop was crowded. I couldn't see either Gaby or Melanie. There was, however, an arrow pointing to an exhibition of Eskimo sculpture and, knowing Gaby's fondness for the birds and beasts and squat muffled people which the Eskimos carve, I started in that direction.

Suddenly there was a violent commotion.

A couple of women seemed to be struggling together in one of the aisles. The younger, dressed in slacks and an anorak, looked like a student. She was hanging on grimly to the older woman who was attempting to free herself. The older woman wore a dark fur coat and a reddish hat.

Melanie. I caught my breath. Melanie involved in some brawl. It couldn't be. No, I thought desperately, no! But it was actually happening.

"Thief!" cried the girl in the anorak. "Help me hold her. She's a thief."

"How dare you! How dare you!" the woman said loudly. "Let me go at once."

I expelled my breath slowly. It wasn't Melanie. Thank God it wasn't Melanie. That was all I cared about at the moment, that and collecting Gaby and Melanie and getting out of the place; I must admit I didn't waste any pity on the poor wretch whom I had mistaken for my sister.

I spotted Gaby first, at the further end of the shop. Melanie was standing close beside her. And immediately I was reassured. I couldn't understand how I had been so stupid as to confuse my sister with that other woman, who was older and plumper and altogether more matronly; in fact the resemblance was superficial. Relief flooded through me.

A circle of curious shoppers had formed almost instantly around the accused and the accuser and my way to Gaby and Melanie was blocked. I stood and watched, like everyone else; but impatiently. I was still eager to get out of the shop. This business was nothing to do with me and I didn't want to get mixed up in it.

The matron's face was the colour of her hat—plum rather than the brighter red that Melanie was wearing—and she was very near to tears. She had been indignant but her indignation was turning to fear; she wasn't used to violent treatment. Her aggressor, sensing a moral victory, had let her go but was still threatening.

"She took some of those brooches. I saw her!" she declared triumphantly. "She put them inside her coat. She's a thief. I—I'm going to get the police."

The spectators parted to let the girl go. No one tried to stop her. They were mostly office workers from nearby government departments. Honest themselves, they didn't have much sympathy with shop-lifting matrons and they were a little titillated by the excitement.

The girl hurried by me in the narrow gangway between the tables piled with bright merchandise. I stood back to let her pass. And I caught a glimpse of a pretty face, an uptilted nose, dark hair concealed under the hood of the anorak and blue eyes which widened in alarm as they looked straight at me. Then she had turned away her head and was running from the shop.

My reactions were slow. I suppose I should have run after her but what would I have said? Haven't we met before? Yesterday, at my press conference, when you asked me silly questions about the Arts Centre Ball and my sister. You were wearing an auburn wig, do you remember? Or perhaps you're naturally a red-head and you're wearing a wig now. But it was no crime to change the colour of one's hair; girls did it all the time. She could have laughed at me or complained to the police.

Besides, I might have made a mistake. I had only seen her briefly and, after my confusion of Melanie with the unfortunate matron, I wouldn't have sworn that the girl in the anorak, and the red-haired journalist were one and the same. And even if they were the same? Was it important? Did it matter to me? When she came back—but I didn't believe she would come back because I was almost positive that she had recognized me and had been afraid.

Anyway, now the manageress had arrived. Summoned from the back of the premises by one of the assistants, she was obviously not pleased with the situation.

"What's this? What's this? Ladies, please move aside." Her voice was sharp with annoyance. "What has happened here?"

The assistant said: "A girl—a student, I think—said she saw that lady steal some brooches. She—she went for the police."

"I didn't do it," the matron cried. "I haven't taken anything."

She sounded slightly hysterical and this time I looked at her with pity—and curiosity. She could be telling the truth. At the moment it was her word against the supposed redhead's. If it really had been Melanie . . .

"I didn't do it," she repeated on a higher note of shrillness. "I haven't taken anything. I'm *not* a thief."

"One moment!"

Everyone turned to look at the man. He was of medium height, broad-shouldered and dark, and at a jaunty angle on his unusually round head he wore a tall astrakhan hat. In one hand he held a pair of felt boots appliquéd with scarlet flowers and in the other an ookpik—an owl-doll made of sealskin—which he waved commandingly. They didn't detract from his authority in the least.

"Ma'am, are you sure you're not making an error of judgment?" He addressed the manageress. "I was standing close by and I'm positive this lady didn't steal or attempt to steal anything. Everyone seems prepared to condemn without any evidence."

"Someone saw her," the manageress said, "and there has been a lot of pilfering lately."

"Someone said she saw her," he corrected. "And that person has disappeared. She made a charge which everyone accepted without question, and then she went to get your CFP. But she hasn't returned and no police officer has arrived. I'd guess that if there has been any pilfering today, she's the most likely suspect."

There was a murmur of assent among the bystanders, a muttering, a shift of sympathy. Some of them probably felt a little ashamed. A stool was produced and offered to the matron. The manageress was nonplussed.

"I—I don't know what to say," she said. "Perhaps you'd come into the office, madam."

"No, no, I don't think I will." Courage had returned with the moral support which she had been offered. She stood up and opened her coat. "You can see for yourself. I have no pockets, nowhere to put the objects you accuse me of stealing. And they're not in here." She opened her handbag and held it out for anyone's inspection; no one looked in it.

"I'm sorry," the manageress said. "Obviously there has been a misunderstanding. That student hasn't come back. Perhaps she was playing some sort of joke."

"A joke!" The matron was outraged. "I should prosecute you for defamation of character," she said. "I may yet— my brother-in-law's a lawyer."

With this Parthian shot she gathered her coat around her and made for the door. The manageress followed her, still apologizing. The man who had intervened—an American by his accent—went up to an assistant and asked if he might buy the felt boots and the ookpik. The excitement was over.

I hurried to join Gaby and Melanie, who were talking to another assistant. Gaby had seen me and waved.

"Hello, darling," she said, "I'm so glad you're here."

"Yes," I said. "Let's go, shall we?"

"In a minute," she said. "I've not looked at the new prints from Cape Dorset yet. I waited for you."

"Can't we leave them till another day?"

"No. They'll all be sold. And you know I promised Colette. She'll be so disappointed."

Colette's our only child. Married at seventeen, she lives in Jersey, in the Channel Isles, absurdly happy and at the moment absurdly pregnant. She had asked us to get her an Eskimo print to match the one we had already sent her. "Oh very well," I said grudgingly, "but we must be quick. I've a—a telephone call to make."

We followed the assistant into one of the bays where the prints were kept in wide, shallow drawers. There were only six of the new lot by the family of Pitseolak and she held them up one by one for our inspection.

Almost any other time I'd have been fascinated but now I could only bless Gaby for being so decisive.

"That's it, isn't it Mark?" she said, immediately she saw the last, which was of a flock of birds watched from a corner of the picture by an Eskimo boy. The birds were of no particular species, the boy a mere outline; it was a master-piece of abstraction. "I'll have that one, please. I think it's beautiful and I'm sure my daughter'll love it."

She went off with the assistant to pay for the print and

have it packed. Melanie began to talk about the shop-lifting incident but I told her to shut up until we had left *The Canada Goose*. She gave me an odd look but didn't argue. Nor did she refer to it again before we got to the Rolls, except to draw my attention to the police—the same CFP men as I had seen earlier—when we were hurrying along the Mall; obviously the girl in the anorak hadn't gone near them.

But once in the car Melanie couldn't contain herself. "Wasn't that an extraordinary business in that shop?" she said. "It didn't make any sense."

"It was rather horrible," Gaby said. "We were all ready to throw stones at that poor woman or watch them being thrown. Mark, I thought you would—but you didn't. I suppose it was difficult for you."

She didn't have to explain more articulately; I knew what she meant.

"I'm sorry," I said.

Melanie, who had no qualms about her own behaviour, said: "The woman was lucky anybody was prepared to stand up for her. And she didn't even say thank-you to Astrakhan Hat."

"Who?"

"Oh, the American who came to her rescue. Surely you noticed the lovely fur hat he was wearing. I wonder who he is."

"I've no idea. But I did recognize the girl in the anorak. She was at the press conference yesterday. She asked a couple of questions."

"Are you sure?" Gaby asked.

"Not absolutely," I said.

"People do look alike," Gaby said. And suddenly she grinned. "You know, for one awful moment when I heard the rumpus and came out of the sculpture exhibition to see what was happening, I thought it was Melanie whom the girl was hanging on to."

"Me!" Melanie was horrified. "You mean you took that woman for me?"

"Yes. You were much the same height and both wearing mink coats and reddish hats. It was only for an instant."

"I should jolly well hope so. She was at least ten years

older than me and fatter and—"

"I had exactly the same impression," I said grimly.

Gaby, who had begun to laugh at Melanie's indignation, stopped abruptly. "Mark, surely not," she said. "It must be a coincidence—mustn't it?"

"I wish to God I knew," I said.

"What on earth are you talking about?" Melanie demanded.

"It seems to me quite probable," I said slowly, "that it was you the girl intended to accuse of shop-lifting. She was going to make a big scene, call the CFP and then disappear. It would've been a choice news item: Dr. Melanie Lowrey, sister of the British Ambassador, accused of pilfering in *The Canada Goose*. But she only had a description of you and she got the wrong woman."

"But, Mark, that's crazy," Melanie protested. "Why should she do such a wild thing? You said she was a journalist, a reputable one presumably, if she was at your press conference. She wouldn't manufacture news for her paper."

I hesitated. Until I had consulted Woods-Dawson it was difficult to know how much to explain to Melanie.

Gaby solved the problem. She said succinctly: "There are a lot of people who dislike the Brits, as they call us here. They'd wave flags if the Ambassador's eminent sister indulged in a spot of shop-lifting."

Melanie glared at her. "You don't have to be so bloody whimsical about it," she said. "It wouldn't do my reputation at Oxford any good either. My God, what a thought! Mark, I can't believe it. It's much too far-fetched."

"No, I don't think so," I said. "Gaby has been telling all our friends and acquaintances how much Colette liked that Pitseolak print we sent her and how eager she was to get another one for her. Anyone who wanted could have found out that a new consignment of prints had arrived and guessed that you'd be in the shop this morning. The rest would have been easy—if there hadn't been a mix-up."

I don't usually drink spirits before lunch but today was an exception. The first thing I did when I got into the study was to pour myself a stiff whisky and soda. Then I dialled transatlantic and got through to Woods-Dawson.

To my surprise he was neither angry nor unduly perturbed at what I had to tell him, even though it was Melanie who was involved. But he was interested, extremely. He went through my story with a small-tooth comb until at last I had persuaded him that he knew as much about the incident as I did.

"Well, they ballsed that one up all right," he said with satisfaction.

"You do think that the whole thing was a plant, then?"

"No doubt at all." He was positive. "The girl would've sent in the police and we'd have had some very unpleasant publicity. People always believe the worst on the no smoke without fire principle. But once she'd seen you and realized you were taking no action she knew she must've made a mistake. If it had been your sister you wouldn't have let the girl walk out of the shop knowing she was going to the CFP, would you?"

"No," I agreed, "I suppose not."

"So we were lucky—this time. But don't let's delude ourselves, Mark. There are going to be more incidents. And sooner or later they'll fit together in some sort of pattern."

"You don't encourage me."

"At least none of you are in any physical danger at the moment. I'm sure of that. They don't want to make a martyr of you, remember. They just want to make you bloody unpopular."

"Jolly!"

Woods-Dawson laughed. "Vigilance at all times, dear boy. That's what's needed."

"Yes," I said bitterly. "You've convinced me." And indeed he had; for the first time his concept of a conspiracy had become real to me.

There was a long pause and I expected him to say goodbye and ring off but when he spoke again I sensed that his interest had suddenly quickened. Something had excited him.

"Mark, if you'd had to plan the scenario in the shop what would you have done differently?" he wanted to know.

I made various suggestions but he vetoed the lot. In the

end I was forced to ask, which pleased him. I caught the edge of his satisfaction.

"Dear boy, it's so obvious once you've hit upon it. The girl should have planted something—a brooch or whatever—on your sister. She could have done easily. Then the whole scene would've become much more important. The bad publicity would've quadrupled. So why didn't she?"

"God knows," I said. "I suppose those weren't her orders."

"Are you absolutely certain she didn't?"

"Not absolutely. But she accused the woman of putting the brooches in her coat and the woman certainly had nothing there. She opened her coat to demonstrate. She had no pockets or means of hiding anything. She offered her handbag too, though I don't believe anyone looked in it."

"Well, that's fascinating. Why didn't she?" Woods-Dawson asked, so softly that I barely caught the words. "If only we knew the answer to that, Mark..."

Yes, indeed. If only we had known the answer to that, what a lot of trouble and heartache we should have been saved.

CHAPTER 4

December 19, evening

IN THE EVENING we went to Walter Eland's cocktail party.
I can't pretend I had been looking forward to it. Walter's
parties, as I remembered them from London, were usually
large, amorphous affairs for which he paid the bill and
bought the liquor. The caterers provided everything else,
from standard soft drinks to standard hot snacks, from plain
paper napkins to anonymous maids and even, one could
imagine, some of the guests, who were apt to be a dreary,
ill-assorted collection. The result was seldom memorable.

I realized, however, as soon as we were inside the apartment, that this party was to be different. There was a mass
of flowers on the hall table and more in the living-room.
The crowd was gay, lively and well-dressed, and the roar
of conversation and the spontaneous laughter were sure signs
that everyone was enjoying themselves—everyone except
the host.

Walter was standing near the doorway, pulling at his
moustache and regarding his guests morosely, as if he were
thinking that they would have been perfectly happy without
him and he didn't care a damn about them. But when he
caught sight of us, or rather of Melanie, his long, rather
lugubrious face lit up with pleasure and I guessed that it
was for her benefit he had made such a special effort; I
hoped she would show her appreciation.

He came to greet us and I apologized for being late.

"It's good of you to come at all, Mark," he said. "It's an imposition for your friends to ask you to this sort of party when you've so many duty invitations."

"Nonsense, Walter dear! There are some people we always enjoy visiting and you're one of them," Gaby said untruthfully, kissing him on the cheek. "And your flat looks lovely. What glorious flowers! You've been wildly extravagant."

Melanie offered him her hand. "Very nice," she said, which seemed an inadequate reward for the trouble he had taken but she was in a sour mood.

"I hope you saw the correction in tonight's paper," Walter said.

"What correction?" Melanie asked.

"Oh damn! You didn't see it then." Walter was annoyed. "The correction to that photograph caption which should have read: Dr. Melanie Lowrey was partnered at the National Arts Centre Ball by Mr. Walter Eland, not by Mr. John Coller. I called the editor and asked him to print an *erratum*. It was in tonight, but buried in the copy so nobody's going to notice it."

"Well, it doesn't matter," Melanie said. "It wasn't important."

"It was to me," Walter said. "I'd have liked the credit for being your partner. My stock would have gone up no end."

We all laughed. Our drinks came, Walter took Melanie away to introduce her to someone and Gaby and I joined another group, which included a charming secretary from the French Embassy.

"Canada could have been the most wonderful country in the world," she was saying. "She could've had American technology, English government, and French culture. *Mais hélas,* she has English technology, French government and American culture."

There was general laughter. It wasn't a new story but it wasn't often told so expressively and with such an attractive accent. The men were appreciative, the ladies envious.

A French-Canadian said: "Madame, as a good Québecois I should take umbrage but with you I cannot disagree."

"Gallic gallantry, monsieur, is obviously the same on both sides of the Atlantic," she answered prettily.

"Then that leaves it up to Toronto," another man said. "And as a good Anglo-Saxon character myself I do take umbrage with the lady. When you consider what the Brits are doing up in the North with their Carmine Project I don't think we've got any right to complain about English technology, even if the money does come from the States. What do you say, Ambassador?"

I said: "I'm grateful for your faith in British technology, but you're wrong about the money. The Americans have nothing to do with the Project at all."

"Ah, but I heard you on the TV," he persisted.

No one else was interested in a serious discussion on Carmine. The group reformed, leaving me to argue—or rather to listen. This particular Torontonian, who said he was a Senator Portman, knew it all; what his pals on Bay Street hadn't told him he had learnt from my press conference. He was a mine of misinformation, which he hadn't the slightest desire to rectify. I did try because it's people like him who spread false rumours, but I soon gave up the attempt. Whatever I said he was going to misquote.

He had me backed up against one of those room-dividers—free-standing shelves filled with books and ornaments—and was obviously looking forward to a long chat with his new chum, the British Ambassador. But I had other ideas and I was just about to make my move when I was startled by voices directly behind me, on the other side of the room-divider.

"Hello, Melanie. Has the faithful Walter deserted you?"

"Sally—good evening. That's a very pretty dress you're wearing."

"I think it's g-gorgeous myself. But, my dear, it's like a skin. I can't wear a thing underneath except my body stocking and the metallic thread tickles. It makes me feel wicked."

Sally Stocker gave a wild giggle. And I realized with sudden alarm, that she was more than half-way tight.

"Alex was furious about it. He said it was indecent and he didn't want his wife showing all she'd got to a lot of sodding diplomats or words to that effect. We had an absolutely ghastly row before we came out tonight."

"Which you won."

"I did?"

"Well, you didn't change your dress."

"No. Poor old Alex. It's his frightful job. He worries all the time about putting up a black. Lowrey makes his life hell. Oh Mel—sorry! I forgot H.E. was your brother. But he *is* an unmentionable so-and-so all the same."

I felt the anger flame in my face and blessed the fact that my Toronto acquaintance was too absorbed with his own spiel to have absorbed Sally Stocker's drunken remarks. I looked him straight in the eye, interrupted what he was saying to tell him how much I had enjoyed our conversation, apologized for having to leave him and, still talking, made my escape.

I looked around for Gaby and found her chatting to Edgar King. As I joined them I heard her mention the snow-mobiling party which the Kings were giving the next day. But it seemed that wasn't a subject that Edgar wanted to discuss, at least not with me. I suppose he thought I might start to cross-question him about the high-paid Presidential help whom he was so eager for me to meet; perhaps Heather oughtn't to have said anything about it. At any rate he gobbled at me like an unhappy turkey and at last managed to speak.

"Excuse me, will you? I must get another drink."

"That was rather sudden, wasn't it?" I said to Gaby as Edgar left us.

"Yes, it was rather. He's a bit drunk, I think. Mark!"

I felt the pressure of her fingers on my arm and followed the direction of her gaze to where Walter was talking to a new arrival, a dark, broad-shouldered man with a round head.

"You recognize him?" Gaby asked softly.

"Yes, of course, the American who came to the matron's rescue in *The Canada Goose* this morning," I said.

"Yes. Astrakhan Hat, as Melanie called him." She laughed. "Maybe now we'll find out what his real name is."

"I'm sure we can if we want to," I said.

I wasn't really interested. Someone nudged me sharply

in the small of the back and I stood aside to let whoever it was pass. But Sally Stocker didn't pass. She hovered between Gaby and myself, swaying gently. She too was looking in the direction of the American.

"Oh boy!" she said to nobody in particular. "But he's a male with some hair on his chest. I think I'll go."

I didn't realize her intention until too late. I was still wondering what to do about her when she pushed past us and a few other people, who were in her way, and ran towards Walter and the American, calling: "John! John!" She had almost reached them when she tripped. She would have fallen if the American hadn't caught her. He righted her decorously but she clung to him and he had to keep his arm around her to support her. Someone laughed unkindly; the little scene was not escaping attention.

"Damn the woman!" I said. "First the trouble with the dress shop and now this."

I saw Alex, unaware of his wife's behaviour, chatting up a couple of women, and went across to him. I caught him by the sleeve and turned him round so that he could take in what was happening. I heard my own voice, quiet and dispassionate, a most unreliable indicator of my feelings.

"Alex, your wife is drunk and she's making a nuisance of herself. Get her out of here, please. Now!"

He didn't say anything. But every vestige of colour left his face and his eyes as he glared at me became unfocused. He jerked his arm free.

"Now!" I repeated. "Get her out of here."

"Alex, dear." Gaby had followed me. "Sally does need you."

He expelled his breath slowly, nodded at Gaby, turned on his heel and went. Gaby sighed with relief.

"Thank God," she said. "Oh, Mark—you shouldn't have spoken to him like that."

"Why not?" I demanded.

"Because he adores Sally and he's going to be so hurt and angry. Besides, there must be something wrong. Sally doesn't usually drink too much."

"They've had a row about that damn dress she's wearing.

It's probably not even paid for and it makes her look like a tart. She's been behaving like one too." I was still seething; didn't Gaby understand? "For God's sake, Gaby, the British can't afford scenes at top-level Canadian parties. You know how this'll get blown up."

Gaby said coldly: "You lost your temper. It was lucky Alex just managed not to. He was within a hair's breadth of hitting you. If he had, that would certainly have set the tongues wagging. And it would've been largely your fault. I—I don't think you realize how short-tempered you've been lately, Mark."

I was learning some home-truths about myself this evening, I thought bitterly. It seemed I was an unmentionable so-and-so at work and bad-tempered at home. If the strain of being British Ambassador in Ottawa was already telling on me so much I wouldn't stay the course; Woods-Dawson had backed the wrong horse.

"I'm sorry, darling," I said. "Truly. Let's not quarrel over it. I couldn't bear it." I sighed; my anger had evaporated. "And I'll try to be better tempered."

She smiled at me ruefully. "I'm sorry too, darling. I'm somewhat fraught myself. What with that unpleasant affair in *The Canada Goose* this morning and now Sally, it's been a horrid day, hasn't it?"

"It has," I agreed, happily ignorant that the day had still more unpleasantness in store.

At this point Heather King and another couple joined us and we chatted about trivialities. Across the room I saw that Melanie was with Walter and the American. As I looked in their direction she signaled to me and, excusing myself, I went over to them. The Stockers, thank God, had disappeared. I would give them five minutes and we would follow. I wasn't enjoying Walter's party in the slightest and nor, I was sure, was Gaby. Melanie, on the contrary, now seemed in good form.

She greeted me with a wide smile; something had amused her.

"Mark," she said, "you'll never guess who this gentleman is."

"Other than Astrakhan Hat," the American said. "Mr.

Ambassador, it's an honour to meet you, sir."

He grinned at me as we shook hands. He had a very attractive grin and a firm handshake. I liked him.

"I recognized you even without the hat," I said.

"Yes. Dr. Lowrey said you were in the store. That poor woman! It wasn't funny for her, was it? I ought've intervened sooner but, you know how it is, one hates to get involved in what could've been a police matter, especially in a foreign country."

"Mark didn't lift a finger," Melanie said.

He gave me an amused, sympathetic glance. "Naturally not," he said. "It's permitted, on occasion, for an attaché to be so stupid as to be rash, but an ambassador must always have more sense. Imagine how embarrassing it would've been if she had stolen those brooches."

"But—but you swore you were standing near her and she couldn't possibly have taken anything," Melanie said.

"I lied," he admitted. "Perhaps I shouldn't have done but when I saw everyone closing in on her, pre-judging her, terrifying her . . . Do you think I was wrong?"

"No!" Melanie shook her head.

"We—ell," Walter said, more sceptical.

The American gave a rueful shrug. "It was a fool thing to do, I know. I hope my ambassador doesn't hear about it. But when I was on vacation in Spain once I saw an old man who'd stolen a piece of meat from a butcher's shop. Some young punks had chased after him and got him cornered. He had exactly the same look as that woman. Which sort of explains my behaviour, even if it doesn't excuse it."

"There's a lot of difference between a hungry man stealing food and a lady pilfering bits of jewellery," Walter protested.

"You've missed the point, Walter," Melanie said sharply. She gave the American her brightest smile. "You don't need an excuse for what you did this morning, Mr. Coller. It was very noble of you."

"Mr. Coller! Not Mr. John Coller?" I said.

"Mr. John Coller, no less—my close friend from Washington." Melanie laughed.

"I'm sorry I didn't give you my name before, Sir Mark,"

he said. "Something came up in our conversation and I got side-tracked.

"My fault," Walter said. "I should've introduced you properly."

"Please," I said. "I was just surprised by the coincidence. I was forgetting what a small place Ottawa is."

"I called the newspaper and gave them hell for their carelessness," Coller said. "Walter did the same, I gather. Of course, I was honoured to have my name linked with Dr. Lowrey's and, if it didn't cause her any inconvenience or embarrassment, I'm quite happy."

"Not a bit," Melanie said. "Why should it?"

"Well, I don't rightly know." He grinned. "But I'm sure Walter wasn't very pleased and the girl from my Embassy whom I'd partnered to the Ball was hopping mad about it. I think she'd have liked her own picture in the paper. Anyway I've been offering apologies all around."

"You have one due to you too," I said. "I'm sorry that on your arrival at Walter's party the British greeting was so—exuberant."

For a moment he looked blank. "Oh, you mean Mrs. Stocker? You mustn't worry about that, Mr. Ambassador. It was nothing," he said generously, "the sort of thing that could happen to anyone."

Gaby joined us then and there were more introductions and explanations. But I was quick to seize my opportunity. With my wife, my sister and my host all in the same place it was too good a chance to miss, especially as the Stockers would be well away by now. I told Walter we had to go.

He did his best to persuade us not to, pointing out that there would be a cold buffet and he had been hoping... Gaby said we were very sorry; Walter must visit us soon. John Coller had made his farewells and tactfully drifted away; out of the corner of my eye I noticed that he had gone to talk to Edgar King. Walter then suggested that Melanie at least should stay; he promised he would drive her home himself. Melanie hesitated, either tempted or touched by Walter's disappointment, but decided she was feeling tired. Walter didn't press her.

He was a little stiff as he said goodbye to us at the door

and my conscience pricked me. It wasn't until we were in the car that I realized we had been at his party for barely fifty minutes. I wished we had stayed longer; it wasn't Walter's fault the evening had turned out so badly. At best I had been inconsiderate, at worst rude. Metaphorically I kicked myself.

Gaby and Melanie were talking about the party and I turned on the radio in the hope of catching some news; I'm an inveterate news-catcher. Music blared through the Rolls. Hurriedly I turned down the sound and fiddled with the dials. The announcer's voice came through, clear and emotionless.

". . . the wound required ten stitches and the British Trade Commissioner was advised to remain in the hospital overnight. However, he refused and has since returned to his residence in Westmount. That is the end of a news bulletin from your English language station in Montreal."

I switched off the radio.

Gaby said: "Darling, what is it? Something's happened to the Browns?"

"Yes. I'm afraid so."

"What? A car accident?"

"I don't know. I don't think it could've been a car accident. The announcer mentioned a wound. It would be an odd word to use."

"Who are the Browns?" Melanie asked.

I let Gaby explain. I picked up the telephone and put it down again. We would be home in five minutes; it would be better to telephone Brown from the house on a secure line than from the Rolls; five minutes wouldn't make any difference; there was no need to panic. I heard Gaby say: "They're absolute dears—the kindest, most helpful of people."

If she had added "and the most efficient," she would have summed up the Browns perfectly—at any rate Gavin Brown. No one could have asked for a more capable or conscientious Trade Commissioner. But he was fifty-eight, not a young man, and his wife was much the same age; if this was part of Woods-Dawson's supposed pattern and things were going to get rough in Montreal . . .

• • •

For the second time today I hurried into the house, intent on telephoning, and again the first thing I did was to pour myself a whisky and soda—I had had only one at Walter's party. While I sipped the liquor and waited for someone to answer the monotonous ringing, I thought of Edgar King; I had no intention of drowning my troubles in drink as he seemed to be doing these days, but I appreciated how easily it could happen.

"Brown here! Who is it?"

"This is Mark Lowrey. How are you?"

"I'm—fine. Sorry I was so abrupt but we've had a spot of trouble."

"So I heard—on the radio, which is why I phoned. Are you all right?"

"Yes. It's a scratch. But Meg's suffering from shock. She was splendid while the excitement lasted but when we got home she collapsed. The doctor's with her at the moment, giving her a sedative."

"Poor Meg! I'm sorry. And your scratch—ten stitches' worth?"

"Eight!" he laughed. "But there was lots of blood—curse them!"

I swallowed. "Gavin, I only heard the tail-end of a news bulletin. Tell me what happened—now, if you will, or would you rather phone back when the doctor's gone?"

"Now's okay. I'll give you the bare bones and send you a full report as soon as possible." His voice was hoarse. "Mark, you know we've been having a small trade fair in Montreal, small in the sense that it was limited to machinery and equipment of use to countries which have lots of ice and snow, the USSR, Scandinavia, the States because of Alaska, Canada. We come into it because of the new stuff we've produced for the Carmine Project—excellent stuff, most of it. The fair itself has been a big success. But there's been trouble, lots of trouble. We've had pickets outside the hotel all the week, and scuffles in the lobby."

He paused and I asked: "What sort of pickets?"

"Mostly anti-Carmine—anti-British and anti-American. Go home Brits. The Arctic belongs to us. Don't sell our

North. Yanks keep your filthy dollars. That sort of thing. Some of it abusive."

"Was it actually stated that there was US money behind Carmine?"

"Yes, it was. There were some kids passing out leaflets. I stuffed mine in my pocket. If I can find it I'll send it to you. All right?" He sounded very tired.

"Yes. I've got the background. What happened today?"

"The top Canadian gave a fork-lunch at his house. He lives on the Mountain. A bus was laid on for guests but lots of people took their own cars. Coming back we were ambushed—and the Americans."

"What?"

"Some louts were pretending to have a snowball fight. They held up a big Cadillac flying the Stars and Stripes, waved on the next car and stopped us. Like a fool, I stuck my head out of the window to ask what was going on and got a snowball with some broken bottle in it in the face. After that we locked ourselves in and Meg telephoned the CFP. That's all really. The police arrived in the nick of time. In the nick of time for Meg and me—the Americans were already upside down in the ditch." He was breathing heavily. "It was a nasty experience while it lasted—very nasty."

"I'm only thankful it was no worse. Gavin, you ought to be in bed. I'm going to say goodbye now and our love to Meg. I'll telephone on Monday. And of course I'll make an official complaint, though I expect it'll be a waste of effort."

I put down the receiver and swore briefly as Gaby came into the room.

"Mark, are they all right?"

I told her what had happened. If it had been Gaby in that car instead of Meg . . . I cursed Woods-Dawson with his confidence that there was no physical danger. I was going to enjoy getting him up in the middle of the night—it would be about two-thirty London time now—to tell him about our latest interesting "incident." I wondered what he would make of it.

CHAPTER 5

December 20

I SAT IN THE front of the car, beside Edgar. Gaby, Melanie and Heather sat in the back. Behind us the heavy Chrysler pulled a trailer, made especially to carry two snowmobiles, which meant that Edgar had to drive with extra care. It was hot in the car, and airless. I caught myself dozing. I had had a bad night.

I had lain awake for hours, my brain churning the events of the day—the extraordinary business in *The Canada Goose* in the morning, later Walter's party, Sally Stocker, John Coller, and that nasty affair in Montreal. What at last I slept I had ghastly dreams in which real happenings were jumbled and garbled and, in an indescribable sort of way, terrifying. I woke about six o'clock. My heart was thudding. My pyjamas were damp with sweat.

And I was absolutely convinced that I now knew something important—if only I could remember what it was.

As we drove out of Ottawa the half memory continued to tantalize me. My head nodded. Suddenly I remembered; the red-headed journalist . . . Then it was gone again. Heather's voice had broken my train of thought.

". . . What do you say, Mark?"

I knew what I wanted to say but I was too polite; anyway it wasn't her fault. "A dozen snowmobiles!" I said: I had taken in the gist of her remarks. "How big is your lot?"

"Fifty acres, mostly bush but plenty of tracks for snowmobiling," Edgar said, "and less than an hour's drive from downtown Ottawa."

"Fifty acres!" Gaby exclaimed. "And you call it a lot?"

Edgar grinned. "This is a fine big country," he said with pride. "But actually Heather meant a dozen people. There's plenty of space for the skidoos. It's the hut that's small and it's pretty primitive. We can't produce a hot meal for more than twelve."

"You mean it hasn't got all mod. cons?" Melanie said, refusing to be impressed.

"All mod. cons?" Heather was mystified.

Edgar grunted, dismissing Melanie's explanation. He said to me: "Have you heard of Paul Brill, Mark? He's a special assistant to the President."

I gave up any thought of recapturing my elusive memory. "Of course I've heard of him. It's rumoured that he has more influence on the President than the Prime Minister has."

"You're going to meet him shortly. He's—he's a good chap. We were at Trinity—University of Toronto—together. As a matter of fact he's a distant relation on my mother's side. But I don't see much of him these days. He moves in exalted circles. The rumour's right. He is very close to the President—closer than any other English Canadian."

"He has a French Canadian wife though," Heather interrupted. "From Quebec City. She's *très riche* and *très, très snob.*"

"The trouble is you're jealous of Lucille," Edgar snapped unexpectedly. "You'd like nothing better than to be in her shoes."

"If you're implying I wouldn't mind being married to Paul you're absolutely right," Heather snapped back. "He's a doll. And he's got some common sense too. You can't imagine him being content with a Civil Service job. He earns—"

"Just be thankful for my Civil Service job and all it provides for you and the children," Edgar said venomously. "We mightn't always have it."

"What do you—" Heather began.

"Look out!" I said.

Edgar, startled, braked too hard. The road was slippery. The tail of the car slewed. The trailer failed to respond. In slow motion we slid sideways into the snowbank along the gutter. Edgar swore.

"I'm terribly sorry," I said, feeling guilty at the result of my warning. "But you'd have hit that dog. With his white coat he didn't show up against the snow."

"And the dog is an Englishman's best friend. How clever of you to remember that." Edgar gave me a disgusted look. "You mustn't apologize—old boy. Not to me. You can never owe me an apology."

I flushed. I wasn't used to being spoken to in that tone of voice and I hadn't a clue what he was talking about. I said nothing: I watched the mongrel loping down the road and thought how upset Gaby would have been if we had killed it. I didn't regret having shouted at Edgar in the slightest.

Nevertheless, when he got out of the car to see what damage had been done, I would have followed him; but Heather put a hand on my shoulder.

"Sorry, Mark," she said. "It was my fault. I shouldn't have riled him. We're going through a bad patch at the moment. Edgar's due for a posting but it doesn't come up somehow."

Such an admission from Heather was touching. I patted her hand. "Not to worry," I said inadequately, thinking that in his present state Edgar was no fit emissary to send to any country.

Edgar returned. "Just another dent or two," he said, sounding morose. "Luckily there's a truck behind. The driver's going to give us a hand. He's got some gravel."

He put his foot lightly on the gas pedal and the car pulled away slowly. The tyres spun on the icy surface as the weight of the trailer held us back. The engine screamed its protest. Then we were away. Edgar hooted his thanks to the truck and I saw Heather give Gaby and Melanie a weak smile.

To relieve the tension Gaby asked who else, besides ourselves and the Brills, was making up the snowmobiling party and Heather began to describe her other guests. The last name she mentioned was that of John Coller.

"John Coller!"

Melanie, who had spent most of the drive gazing out of the car window at the flat snow-covered landscape, was pleased. There was real interest in her voice, which amused me. Three days ago we had never heard of John Coller and now we couldn't get away from him. If this went on he would almost begin to qualify as the close friend of Melanie's that the newspaper . . .

Suddenly I remembered what I had known with such certainty during the night and what had been niggling at my mind ever since like a half-forgotten tune. My casual thoughts collapsed over a a precipice.

At my press conference the red-headed journalist had asked me about John Coller's relationship with Melanie. She had used the phrase "a close friend" and I had assumed that she had taken it from the paper and that her second question was as innocently stupid as the one which had led up to it, the one about Gaby and myself not going to the Arts Centre Ball. But the girl who had tried to accuse my sister of shop-lifting wouldn't ask innocent, stupid questions.

So now I knew. The communist plan which was concerned with me, the British Ambassador—and I was convinced, after yesterday, that there was some such plan— was also concerned with John Coller. I wondered if Woods-Dawson realized that I had a potential ally.

Without my noticing we had left the highway. Now we turned off the concession road on to a dirt track bordering the Kings' property and, after about a hundred yards, parked near a gate. On it, his crash helmet pushed to the back of his head, was sitting John Coller. He looked as if he hadn't got a care in the world. I wondered how much this was a façade.

But it was no time for brooding. Everyone had arrived or was arriving. There were salutations and introductions. I had to be civil. Besides, there was work to be done. Snowmobiles had to be unloaded off the trailers. Food and churns of drinking water had to be unpacked from the Chrysler and then repacked on the biggest and heaviest snowmobile. Equipment had to be checked. When we were almost ready Edgar put on snowshoes.

"We can't get all the stuff on one machine," he said, "so I'm going ahead with a pack. You'll find me at the hut lighting a fire. Heather'll show you the way. Please follow her and stick to the track."

We chorused our goodbyes as Edgar set off. He had left us very little to do. Soon Heather was nosing her skidoo through the gate and we had begun the hard, bumpy ride to the hut. It was a most uncomfortable journey. The combined noise of the engines was overpowering, great powdery blobs of snow fell on us from overhead branches, ice-covered brambles slashed at our faces, and the rutted track jolted our bodies unmercifully. It was not an auspicious introduction to snowmobiling.

However, within ten minutes we had reached the large clearing in which the hut stood and, once the engines were switched off, we could appreciate the beauty and peace of the Canadian bush in winer. The sun shone from a deep blue sky on virgin snow, the tall dark trees sparkled with frost and the air was cold and pure and invigorating. Except for the line of orange monsters which had brought us we could have been a thousand miles from civilization. Even Gaby managed a cheerful smile.

Edgar came out of the hut to help carry in the rest of the food and the drinking water. He said—and I sensed he wasn't altogether joking—"I was hoping you'd all get lost and I could stay here alone for ever. God, it was wonderful when I shooed into the clearing. Utter bliss!"

"I'm glad you remembered to light the fire," Heather said sarcastically.

"Oh yes," Edgar said. "I faced up to reality very quickly. The fire's going and there's water on the stove. Come along in, everyone."

We crowded into the hut and huddled around the fire which wasn't giving off much heat yet. As Edgar leaned over me to poke the logs I realized that in addition to his duties he had found time for a stiff whisky. To be honest, after the ride in, I wouldn't have minded one myself. But there was no opportunity; only coffee was provided.

Heather looked at her watch. "We should go soon if we're to get a good run before lunch."

"Right!" Edgar took the hint. "I'm afraid I'll have to organize you all for safety's sake. Some of you don't know the terrain and some of you can't drive. Also our British friends have never done any snowmobiling before. They must be looked after and shown what a good sport it is. So I'm going to pair you off. Okay?"

There was a murmur of assent. I wanted to laugh. It was a reasonable arrangement but heavy-handed. Paul Brill and I would have made more contact with each other across a dinner table than roaring over the snow. But maybe Edgar had other fish to fry; perhaps the scientist from the Defence Research Board was to be charmed by Mme. Brill or perhaps Edgar had plans for the Brigadier.

On one count at least I must have been wrong. Gaby was assigned to the Brigadier, which was a relief to me. It meant I didn't have to worry about her. He was an expert snowmobiler and at worst would bore her by a replay of the Toronto Maple Leafs beating the Boston Bruins on their home ice. As for Melanie, I had been able to judge for myself on the ride from the gate that John Coller was an excellent driver; she would enjoy herself. I hoped to do the same. If I could relax and blow away a few of the cobwebs I would be in better shape to do some constructive thinking later. Content enough, I climbed into the back of Paul Brill's skidoo.

"Everybody meet at the mound," Edgar shouted. "But make your own way there."

"Back at the hut by one-thirty," Heather added. "Steaks for lunch."

There was a ghastly, peace-shattering screech as six snowmobile engines started up together. But when the vehicles moved off, each taking a different course, the noise decreased until conversation was possible. Paul Brill, however, showed no inclination to talk.

We skimmed smoothly over the white-crusted earth, winding our way through thickets heavy with snow, and the only sound to disturb the silence was the staccato phut-phut of our machine. Nevertheless, I rather wished we could have been on snowshoes, even though I suspected that snowshoeing was not as easy as Edgar made it appear. Snowmobiling seemed to me to have few advantages.

I changed my mind, however, when we reached the mound. The mound was, in fact, a hillock in the middle of an undulating, snow-covered area, surrounded by firs and pines. Free of bush, this was more than an acre in size and an ideal place for snowmobiling. For ten minutes we zoomed around, sometimes flying through the air as skis and tracks lost contact with the ground. It was a wildly exhilarating experience. I was sorry when my driver switched off the engine and coasted to a stop.

"Shall we stretch our legs?" he suggested.

"Yes," I agreed and clambered out of the vehicle. "We seem to be the first arrivals."

"Yes. I hope you enjoyed the ride?"

"I did indeed—especially the last part. It was terrific."

"Good."

There was silence. We had run out of conversation.

"What's that spoor over there?" I asked. "Rabbit?"

"Fox, more likely."

There was another, longer silence.

Paul Brill gave me a quizzical smile. "I'm merely an aide to the President, Sir Mark," he said. "You can't expect me to have a diplomat's finesse. Besides, the others'll be here soon. So I'm going to be blunt. Edgar gave me to understand that you wanted to meet me—unofficially. It was his main reason for arranging this little party today. I wondered if perhaps you might have an unofficial message for the President?"

I hid my surprise. I said blandly: "I should hate to mistake a fox for a rabbit again."

Paul Brill laughed and shook his head. "I'm no fox," he said. "But I won't vouch for Edgar."

"Edgar gave me to understand that it was you who was eager to meet me," I said. "But I must admit it never occurred to me that you might have an unofficial message for Her Majesty."

Brill frowned. "It's beyond me," he said. He sounded

annoyed. "But I apologize, Sir Mark."

"What for?" I asked.

He shrugged. "I feel I've been discourteous to you."

"Not at all," I said. "I'm delighted we've met. When I do have an unofficial message for your President I'll get in touch with you."

"Do that—please." He gave me a long look, which was impossible to interpret. "You'll be more than welcome." He pointed to the distant trees from which a snowmobile had emerged. "I recognize that big skidoo. This'll be the Brigadier and your very beautiful wife."

"On Gaby's behalf—thank you."

"I mean it, most sincerely. Even under a crash helmet that long, thin face is pure Pre-Raphaelite."

The remark pleased me immensely and, I realized, coloured my liking for Paul Brill. I repeated it to Gaby as we watched the Brigadier take Brill for a flying ride on his powerful machine. Gaby was amused.

"I thought you'd be discussing more important things than my unfashionable looks," she said.

"We did," I said. "Or I believe we did. Our conversation wasn't exactly pellucid. Between you and me, darling, I really don't know what it was all about."

A snowmobile roared up beside us. Edgar, red in the face from a mixture of cold and alcohol, wanted to know if we were enjoying ourselves. There had been no danger but he had come close enough to throw up the snow at our feet and make Gaby flinch. I put my arm around her.

I said, somewhat stiffly, that Gaby was getting chilled and would like to go back to the hut. Edgar wasn't sympathetic—I suppose he thought we were being spoil-sports—but he promised to arrange it and shot away with such violence that he nearly dislodged his passenger.

"He's drunk, Mark," Gaby said.

"Yes, damn him!" I said. "I suspect he has been nipping from a flask all the morning. I'm not looking forward to him driving us home. But at least I can cope with the car— if not with one of those orange monsters. Right now we're stranded and you're freezing."

"Not really, darling. I'm all right," Gaby said and belied it by shivering. "Anyway here are the Brigadier and Mr. Brill to the rescue."

In fact she was over-optimistic. The Brigadier stopped only long enough for Paul Brill to climb out before he roared away again, shouting that he had promised to give Heather a ride but he would be back. It didn't really matter. Brill agreed at once to take Gaby to the hut and I was quite prepared to wait awhile. I wasn't cold and, as Brill said, laughing, I was too conspicuous a figure for the rest of the party to forget me.

I was a conspicuous figure all right. My outer layer of clothing consisted of green corduroy trousers tucked into boots, and a bright blue windcheater. On my head was a yellow crash helmet, provided by Edgar, to match my yellow scarf and gloves. I stood in the snow with a backdrop of trees behind me. I made an excellent target for anyone desiring to shoot me with either a gun or a camera.

Not that it occurred to me for a moment that anyone would—in spite of what had happened to the Browns and in spite of Woods-Dawson's warnings. It was later that I wondered why he hadn't shot at me then, why he had waited until Melanie and Coller joined me.

For a while I strolled up and down, watching the five snowmobiles; everyone had finally arrived at the mound. People waved as they zoomed past but no one offered to join me. I felt bored and a little lonely. Edgar had clearly forgotten his promise to arrange a lift and the Brigadier was too busy showing off his prowess as a snowmobiler to re-member me. I would have liked nothing better than to have walked back to the hut by myself but the snow was too deep for walking and I didn't know the way.

I was really grateful when John Coller drew up beside me. He switched off the engine and he and Melanie both climbed out of the skidoo. A glance at my sister was enough to tell me that she at any rate was having a good time. She exuded well-being; in fact she looked more relaxed and happier than I had seen her for ages.

She said: "John insisted we should come and talk to you. He said you were being neglected."

"Kind of him."

"To be honest, Sir Mark, I've had enough. Skidooing may be good for the liver but I've got a trick spine and that jolting and bumping plays the devil with it. I ought to buy a heavier machine. You don't notice—hell!"

He had slipped and sat on his bottom. Melanie laughed. He put out a hand and I pulled him to his feet. For a couple of seconds, no more, we stood together, Coller and I, our hands clasped.

The photograph showed us shaking hands, sealing a bargain. My God, the man hidden in the bushes certainly made the most of his opportunities!

"Thanks," Coller said. "I seem accident prone today. We had quite a spill earlier on. Luckily, no damage done, was there?"

"None," Melanie agreed, going rather pink.

"You were a brave girl," he said, putting his arm around her shoulders, more as a gesture of approbation than affection.

And again the photographer seized his chance. With the aid of a telescopic lens he produced an intimate picture of Melanie and John Coller, with myself looking on in approval.

"What happened?" I asked.

They were going to tell me anyhow; they were both full of it. So I did my best to enjoy it with them. Put baldly it wasn't a very interesting story: Coller had been turning to say something over his shoulder when the skidoo hit a hidden log and spilled him and Melanie into a snowdrift, from which they had extricated themselves with a certain amount of difficulty and, I suspect, some horseplay. I dare say it had been amusing at the time and they made it sound entertaining.

Meanwhile the photographer took three more pictures; if there were others I never saw them. The five which I was to see were excellent; the outlines were sharp and the colour true. The man was clearly a professional.

Moreover, unless he had a companion, his skill wasn't reserved for photography. He was also an expert marksman. He proceeded to give us a demonstration. The first shot hit

Coller's snowmobile, which was about five yards from where we were standing. The bullet struck the metal a glancing blow and ricocheted into the snow.

We stopped talking abruptly. We had sensed rather than seen or heard something. We didn't move.

"What was that?" Melanie asked.

She was answered by three shots in rapid succession. Again we heard nothing but I saw flashes of light from the trees on our left. The first two bullets straddled us. The third threw up the snow at our feet—or that was my impression. We didn't stay to make sure.

Instinctively we dived for safety, floundering through a drift of snow to the protection of the belt of firs behind us. We lay on the ground, breathing heavily. It had been a brief but exhausting scramble, especially as Coller and I had almost had to carry Melanie, whose short legs had threatened to bury her in the drift.

It had been slow, too, and with our bright clothes against the white snow we had been fine targets. But our ex-photographer friend hadn't attempted to fire at us. He had waited until we were nicely under cover. Then he sent his parting shot into the trees above our heads.

A shudder seemed to go through the branches of the particular fir that we were lying under and about half a ton of snow and spikes of ice descended on us. As we gasped and choked and thrust our way out of it the air was blue with our cursing.

The marksman must have been laughing his silly head off.

I staggered to my feet and pulled Melanie up beside me. She was very pale. I expect I was too. I also felt horribly cold, partly because it was chilly where we were, out of the sun, and partly from shock; no one had ever shot at me before. Melanie was shivering and her teeth were beginning to chatter. I hugged her to me.

"It's all right, Melanie. Take it easy. It's all right. Look! Someone must have seen what happened. All the snowmobiles are coming over here. We're quite safe now."

"John," she said and swallowed hard. "He's—he's wounded."

"Wounded?"

"No. No, I'm okay."

There was blood on his hand and on the snow. I couldn't believe it. Whatever else he might have been our joker was an excellent marksman and he hadn't shot one of us either by mistake or on purpose.

"Where were you hit?" I heard the suspicion in my voice.

"I wasn't hit!" He sounded angry. "At least not by a bullet. But I lost my helmet getting under here and a bloody bit of ice has cut my head open. It hurts like hell."

He took time out then to swear, half under his breath, and said: "Sorry. Sorry, Sir Mark. I'm glad he didn't get you."

"He wasn't trying to get me. If he had been he had plenty of opportunity before you came on the scene."

"But—Mr. Ambassador, you're not suggesting he was after me—a non-important attaché?"

"Perhaps you underrate yourself or—"

I was about to suggest that maybe he hadn't intended to get anybody when Melanie gulped. "I'm going to be sick."

I turned her around and held her with her back to us while she vomited. Poor Melanie! The stray thought crossed my mind that this would be something to tell her history professor next term. Coller grinned at me over her bent body and inspected the bloodstained handkerchief which he had been holding to his head.

"It's lucky she's a political scientist," he said. "She'd sure have made a poor doctor!"

I grinned back at him. "Let's get out of here," I said.

By now the snowmobilers had arrived in force. Several of them reached across the drift to help us when we appeared on the edge of the trees, and Edgar plunged in, insisting that Melanie must be carried. They were all chattering, wanting to know what had happened, asking questions.

"I saw you," Heather said. "I saw you. You were standing there, perfectly happy. Then suddenly you dashed into the bush. Why?"

"Someone started taking pot shots at us," I said.

They stared at me incredulously and I looked at them

with interest; after all, someone must have passed along the information that John Coller and I would be at the mound this Saturday morning. But every face reflected amazement and innocent dismay.

Edgar took it as a personal insult. "You mean someone shot at you. Here? On my land?"

"From those trees over there," Coller said, pointing, "but he'll be long gone."

There was another chorus of questions, mostly unanswerable.

"I expect it was a hunter. After rabbits probably. We can't really stop them," Heather said.

"He doesn't have to poach my guests," Edgar said. He seemed relieved. "There might've been a nasty accident."

"I don't think it could've been—" Coller began.

I interrupted. "I'm sure you're right. It was just a careless poacher—hunter, did you call him?—and we panicked rather. I've never been taken for a rabbit before but my instinct was to make for a burrow at top speed. However, no damage—except to Mr. Coller's head."

My inanities and sympathy for Coller distracted them. Heather became practical. And soon we were streaming over the snow on our way back to the hut, where the story had to be retold to Gaby and Paul Brill. This time Coller and Melanie, who had been unusually silent for her, supported what I was beginning to think of as the careless poacher theory. Everyone seemed prepared to accept it, though how many of them believed it, God knows. Coller and I, and probably Melanie, knew it was untrue; Gaby sensed it. And I intercepted a meaningful look from Lucille Brill to her husband. As to the rest of them, there was no means of telling.

Certainly, when the police arrived, the account which we gave them was unanimous. No one wanted any trouble—or publicity.

When the police arrived we were having a good time. There was a splendid fug in the hut. We were warm and dry. Coller's head had been attended to—one of the wives turned out to be a nurse—and he was looking somewhat raffish with a large piece of sticking-plaster on his scalp.

We had eaten our steaks and drunk several bottles of wine. Heather was pouring coffee and Edgar had just produced some brandy. We were all laughing uproariously at a very funny joke which I can't remember now.

The CFP arrived on snowshoes so nobody heard them. The first indication we had of their presence was when there was a thunderous knock on the door and it was thrown back on its hinges. They came in with their guns drawn; they were taking no chances.

"What the hell do you want?" Edgar demanded and was ignored.

"Anyone of you armed?"

We shook our heads.

"Okay. I'll take your word for it but don't none of you move too rapid."

"Look, this is a private party on private land." Edgar tried again. It was a pity he didn't sound sober.

"You Mr. Edgar King?"

"Yes, and I want to know what right—"

"We had a report there'd been some shooting. Where's the British Ambassador, Sir Mark—?" The police sergeant, who was the one doing all the talking, consulted a piece of paper. "Can't read the name."

"I'm Sir Mark Lowrey," I said.

It was as much as I was prepared to volunteer. I was fascinated to know what the joker who had shot at us had told the police; the report must have come from him or from someone to whom he had reported.

"And you're okay?"

"Yes."

"And your sister?"

"I'm Dr. Lowrey. I'm all right too."

"Good." He looked straight at Coller. "You Mr. John Coller of the U.S. Embassy? You been wounded?"

"No."

"You're not Coller."

"I am John Coller, but I'm not wounded."

"Then how come you've got that plaster on your head?"

"I was hit by some ice falling from a tree."

There was a long silence. Disbelief was written plainly

on the police sergeant's face. "Somebody can verify that?" he asked slowly.

"Yes, I can," Melanie said.

"Why should anyone have to verify it?" Coller asked.

They had spoken together.

"Thank you—ma'am." The sarcasm was heavy. "We're just checking up—sir. Every report has to be checked up."

"But it was only an accident," Heather said. "A careless hunter."

The police sergeant held up a huge hand; he was a great hulking chap. "One moment. We'll get your story later. First I want all your names."

"This is pre-prepos-posterous." Edgar stumbled over the word.

"I agree, absolutely preposterous," the Brigadier said.

"Name!" The police sergeant pointed at Paul Brill.

We had goaded him and he was prepared to be nasty. To him we were a party of high-paid help having a drunken orgy—he hadn't missed the empty wine bottles—and he didn't care a damn if we all got shot. But he had his job to do and he was going to do it. He didn't mind how unpleasant he had to be; in fact he could enjoy it.

Paul Brill stood up; he must have realized that the situation was getting out of hand. "Brill. Paul Brill. Here are my credentials."

I've never seen anybody change more quickly. One moment a hard-nosed bully, the next the police sergeant was a small man in an over-sized body. He cringed. He grovelled. He was a revolting sight. I was impressed. Paul Brill obviously had enormous clout.

"Mr. Brill, sir, I'm sorry. I sure didn't know. Am I ever sorry, sir."

Brill's mouth tightened; he felt the other man's shame and he hated his own position. I liked him the more for it.

He said: "This is what happened. Take it down." And he proceeded to repeat the bones of the story that we had told him, which amounted to the careless poacher theory. When he had finished he looked around at us and asked: "I've got it right, haven't I? We're all agreed?"

The ayes had it. Only the scientist from the Defence

Research Board studied the tip of his nose and abstained. John Coller met my glance as he nodded. *D'accord!* We understood each other, neither of us wanted to make a big thing of the incident. I suppose everyone there felt the same way.

The CFP withdrew and more apologies. Heather reheated the coffee and we all had some brandy. But the party was ruined. Everybody wanted to get home—except it seemed, Edgar, who now supplied the anti-climax. Very slowly, without any warning, he crumpled out of his chair on the floor. He was dead drunk.

CHAPTER 6

December 22

SUNDAY WAS TOO short. Monday found me ill-prepared for whatever unpleasant shocks Christmas week might have in store. I didn't doubt there would be some.

Meanwhile, a Monday morning at the Chancery, and business as usual. Even before I had struggled out of the paraphernalia of Ottawa winter clothing and adjusted myself to the eighty degree temperature of my office—the cleaning woman always turned up the thermostat at night and nobody ever remembered to turn it down again—my secretary had telephoned Montreal for me.

"Mr. Brown on the line, Sir Mark. Do you want it taped?"

"Please."

She made the necessary adjustments and I sat down at my desk. The in-tray, I saw, was heaped high. My secretary must have noticed the direction of my gaze because she murmured: "There are several priority telegrams from London, Sir Mark. They're in the red folder."

I nodded my thanks. "Hello, Gavin. How are you—and Meg?"

"Quite all right, thank you, apart from a bruise or two. And Meg says when my stitches are taken out it'll look as if I have a dueling scar, which I've always wanted."

I laughed. "Good."

"What about you, Mark—and this shooting business?"

"Nothing to worry about," I lied, following Woods-

Dawson's instructions. "Just a sick joke." What Woods-Dawson had had to say about the Kings' snowmobiling party was unprintable; he couldn't conceive how I had been such a four-starred fool as to go on such an expedition. "Tell me, did you find that leaflet about the Carmine Project that you said you'd stuffed in your pocket?"

"Yes. I've sent it to you with a full report. It's a scurrilous thing. It as good as states we're only a front for the Americans, who really control the Project. And there's something else."

"What?"

"A neighbour of mine came in yesterday evening to ask if there was anything he could do for us. He'd just heard about our "accident." Mark, he's a corporation lawyer and he knows a lot of people. He warned me that there may be more trouble. He says there's a rumour going around in high circles that the Carmine bases are being made adaptable for military purposes."

"Good God!" I said. "That's a new one."

"Yes, but taken with the gossip about American control it could add up to very big trouble."

"Very big trouble," I exclaimed. "You know how touchy the Canadians are about anything military on their territory—and especially anything that might look like a threat across the Pole to Russia."

"And the Russians themselves might have something to say about it, what's more," Gavin said. "They can't be too happy about exploration so close to their Arctic frontier. And if there were military overtones..."

Left with these uncomfortable thoughts, I asked my secretary to get our Toronto office and began to sift through some of the bumph from London. None of it appeared particularly urgent to me in spite of its classification; it was mostly a succession of progressively more plaintive demands to know what I had done in the last few days to exacerbate the Canadians and why the general situation had deteriorated so suddenly. I didn't have an answer to the what or the why, but I was going to have to produce one.

Meanwhile my call from Toronto had come through. The news was fair. Up to now everything was peaceful; no one at the moment seemed out to get the Brits. Nevertheless, our man there did admit that our popularity rating had slipped and for no apparent reason. There seemed to be an epidemic of anti-British and anti-American fever going around; fortunately, he said, most of the cases were mild.

I was about to say goodbye when he told me he was sending me a memo about the Carmine Project. He wanted confirmation that the United States was not connected with it in any way.

So did I. There were too many rumours linking the Americans with the Project to please me. I was beginning to distrust my own vehement denials of their complicity. It was not impossible, I knew, that I had not been told the truth. Nanny, however, had promised to find out for me.

Warily I asked: "Is there any particular reason for your query?"

"Well, there was that television interview yesterday," he said. "Senator Portman—"

"Who?"

"Senator Portman. He comes from Toronto. He's big business but not very bright. His wife has the money and the influence. They're both extreme right-wing, pillars of the John Birch Society. I—I thought you knew him, sir. He gave the impression you were—chums."

"I think I've met him once, at a cocktail party last Friday. Tell me the worst. What did he say?"

"I can't remember his exact words. He was full of praise for the UK and praise for the Carmine Project but somehow everything he said came out sounding not quite right. He overdid his admiration. He made one sick."

"But how did the Americans come into it?"

"It was implied rather than said. You got the impression that although in theory Carmine was an Anglo-Canadian project, in practice the British had been clever enough to make some sort of deal with the Americans. He was pretty vague, but he more or less quoted you as his authority. He said he'd been chatting to his good friend the British Ambassador and therefore he had it all from the horse's mouth— his phrase, Sir Mark."

I groaned. I could picture the Senator on the box, networked from coast to coast and exuding charm, self-assurance, and misinformation. A thousand denials and contradictions would make no difference now. The damage to Britain's image, to say nothing of mine, was done. And, in part at least, it was my own fault. I should never have let the man corner me at Walter's party.

In the course of the day, to allow for the differences in time zones, I was to speak to the Winnipeg and the Vancouver offices. Their story was much the same. Our prestige in the Prairie Provinces, never very high, had sunk even lower and twice in the course of the past week the Winnipeg office had had to be evacuated because of bomb threats; nothing had been found by the CFP but work had been disrupted. Moreoever, the local news media had not been particularly sympathetic and had stated that the UK was not respecting Canadian sovereignty in the Arctic—as if that justified bomb threats.

And in Vancouver, where we leased a ground-floor apartment as an office, the consul had just been told by the superintendent of the building that when our lease ran out in a month or two the rent would be doubled. Danger money the chap had called it. He had said it was only right that we Brits should pay extra insurance, we were a poor risk. Besides, we could afford it, he had added triumphantly, since we had sold out the Carmine Project to the Yanks. It was not, it seemed, the first time recently that the consul had had to refute similar lies.

All in all it was obvious that the unease of the Office was fully justified although, since many of the facts were still unknown to them, somewhat premature. During the last week or so, right across Canada, there had been a growth of anti-British feeling and Carmine was fast becoming a dirty word. Unfortunately I couldn't conceive of any way to improve the situation. On the contrary, I could foresee it deteriorating still more.

And just when I had reached this sad conclusion, as if to make a prophet out of me, my secretary and the Security Officer came hurrying into my room. The building had to be evacuated immediately. Somebody had telephoned the Canadian Federal Police to say that a couple of fifty-pound bombs had been planted in the British Embassy.

It was after seven when I got home with a briefcase full of documents which had to be read. No bomb had been found but, as in Winnipeg, work had been disrupted and it had taken a good deal of time, as well as effort, to clear up after the CFP's search. I could only hope we weren't going to suffer from a succession of bomb scares. It would be bad for everybody's morale—including mine.

I found Gaby and Melanie and, unexpectedly, Walter Eland either sitting or kneeling on the drawing-room floor; they gave the impression of playing some kind of children's game. But as soon as she saw me Gaby jumped to her feet and came to kiss me.

"Darling, are you all right? We heard about the bombs on the six o'clock news. Did they find anything?"

"No, not a thing," I said. "And I'm all right. But what are you doing on the floor?"

"I've brought you a Christmas present," Walter said.

Suddenly he pounced and in one hand caught a coal-black kitten with a white star on its forehead. Heaven knows where he had got it. The kitten was the spit image of what our late-lamented Thomas must once have been and, in fact, he had already been christened, in best diplomatic sherry, Thomas the Second. I poured myself a whisky and soda and drank to him, wishing him a ripe old age and a more peaceful death than Thomas the First.

The four of them—if you include the kitten—continued to play on the floor. I sat on the sofa, sipping my drink and glancing through the evening paper. It was good to relax, but not with the newspaper, which was full of examples of Anglo-American unpopularity. The editor took a neutral and highly sanctimonious line, being opposed to violence, so he said, in any form. He had however, his own coy sense of humour. The lead editorial was headed: "Ambassador mistaken for rabbit." I threw the paper down in disgust. I wondered if the editor had ever been shot at in sport.

Walter came to sit beside me. "You look done in, Mark."

"I am. I've had one of those days. The bloody bomb scare was the last straw."

"One of those weekends too, to judge by the media."

"Yes."

"Melanie was telling me about the Kings' snowmobiling party. Do you really believe that shooting was an accident? Why should the chap have called the police?"

I shrugged. "Someone's idea of a joke maybe."

"The whole thing seems completely pointless to me—except as more bad publicity for the poor old Brits."

"Yes," I said, ignoring the implied question-mark.

I didn't want to talk about it. I told Walter to get himself another drink and, if he wanted to be kind, to get me one too. I yawned. I felt extraordinarily tired. I would have liked a quick dinner alone with Gaby and then bed, to make love and to sleep. But Walter was obviously going to stay—we owed him something after our treatment of his cocktail party last Friday, and his gift of the kitten—and later I should have to work.

"Thanks," I said as he gave me my glass. "By the way, there's something I've been meaning to ask you. It's about Edgar."

"What about Edgar?"

"Well, he's obviously knocking back the drink pretty heavily at the moment. I wondered if you knew what had started him on this jag—when it began."

I had asked Heather the same question but her answer had been vague. I hoped Walter wasn't going to prevaricate. If he did I couldn't press him. But it had become important to know and this was as good a chance as any to find out.

Slightly reluctantly he said: "Since—since the end of March, beginning of April. He and Heather took some leave in March. They went to Jamaica for a couple of weeks and were both in very good form when they got back. But almost immediately after things began to go wrong—his brother had a dreadful automobile accident and nearly died, his mother made herself ill over it—I don't know. Anyhow it was about then that Edgar took to whisky in a big way."

"That would be before Easter, quite some time ago." I hid my satisfaction.

"Yes, though as you've seen for yourself it's got much worse lately. Mark, why did you want to know—about what started it and when, I mean?"

This was a natural question so I was prepared for it. "I've been worried about him," I said with complete truthfulness. "I wondered if he was in trouble of some kind, if something had happened . . . Whatever the cause, I'm sure he needs help."

"I've tried," Walter said, "but he's as close as a clam."

At this point the houseman came in to interrupt our conversation.

"Excuse me, Sir Mark, but there's a telephone call from Manchester."

Manchester stood for Manchester Square, London—otherwise Woods-Dawson. I excused myself to Walter and went along to the study. I was thankful the call hadn't come through five minutes earlier. Walter had now told me all I wanted to know. Edgar's drinking had started before Easter and that meant it could have nothing to do with me and my affairs. I was ashamed that I had even suspected him of being implicated in any way and more than glad I had never mentioned my suspicions to Woods-Dawson.

As Woods-Dawson usually waited for me to telephone him and as it was about two o'clock in the morning, London time, I assumed he had something important to tell me. Indeed he had—two things to be precise, answers to both questions I had asked him.

"First, Carmine," he said. "I can guarantee there's no American involvement in the Project whatsoever, financial or otherwise. I got it from Himself." Woods-Dawson always referred to the Prime Minister as Himself. "I told him that if he was lying to me I'd see to it that he'd be out of office in six months. And he knows I could do it, too. So you can accept it as gospel, Mark. Carmine is pure Anglo-Canadian. What's more, the Canadians are getting a jolly good deal."

"Fine," I said. "I'm relieved." Which was putting it mildly. This was the best bit of news I had had today.

For a few minutes we talked about the Project and the sudden bad publicity it was getting across Canada and I told him about the bomb scare at the Chancery. Then he turned to my second query, which had concerned John Coller.

"Dear boy," he said. "You do make the oddest friends."

"Not exactly from choice. I explained to you. John Coller and I have been thrown at each other. There have been too many coincidences. I know he's an American, but—"

"But you've begun to suspect him? Bully for you, Mark. Suspect everyone on principle."

"Suspect's not the right word," I said. "I was hoping he might be an ally. After all he's been manipulated just as I have. What's more I think he's aware of it."

"I'm damn sure he is. So don't worry about him. He can look after himself. He's a professional, Mark. He's in CIA, the Central Intelligence Agency! That means he's poison as far as you are concerned. There must be no social contact between you or any member of your family and Coller, and the absolute minimum of official contact. Do you understand?"

"Yes," I said weakly, trying to assimilate this new surprise. "I assume I'm not to tell anyone he's in CIA?"

"Absolutely not!" Woods-Dawson was horrified. "The Americans would be furious if the news leaked through us and my source would never forgive me."

"All right. But does Coller's ostracism have to be so complete? Ottawa's a small place, you know, and the diplomatic—governmental community's even smaller."

"It must be as complete as possible without exciting comment. If Coller's cover were blown and you were known as a chum of his the Canadians would immediately suspect you of conspiring with the Yanks against them." Woods-Dawson's voice came over the telephone urgent and deadly serious; he had dropped his usual drawl. "Do you understand, Mark?"

"Yes. I'll do my best."

"Coller will almost certainly collaborate. He'll have realized he's being used and he won't want any part in a forced friendship with you. I'm told he's one of their best men."

"How nice for them," I said, resenting the implication.

"Too bad the British have to depend on an amateur like me. But after all I was hired as a diplomat."

"Never mind, dear boy," Woods-Dawson said soothingly. "You're learning. And Nanny's here to look after you. Between us we'll keep the old flag flying."

CHAPTER 7

December 23

THE FOLLOWING MORNING, for the first time since Canada had left the Commonwealth, the Chancery was picketed—and "the old flag" was flat. A two-inch snowfall had been swept from the pavement in front of the building and large sheets of heavy paper, painted to represent Union Jacks, had been laid down. On these symbolic flags the pickets walked, up and down venting their spleen and waving placards whose theme, variously expressed, appeared to be Canada for the Canadians and Brits go home.

A score of protesters went around to the sides and back of the building to surround us. But this was our land and I demanded that the CFP disperse them. I could do nothing about the others, almost a hundred in number and mostly young, not even about the boy who stood outside our front doors and handed to every caller a lying leaflet on the Carmine Project, identical with the one Gavin Brown had sent me from Montreal.

I watched them from my office window high above their heads and cursed the lot of them, though I suppose only a handful were communists; the rest were just letting themselves be used. It was a completely futile exercise on my part but it relieved my feelings, which were a mixture of anger and apprehension. The anger subsided as my apprehension grew and I asked myself over and over again if the fact that they had chosen today for their demo had any significance.

Today was the day of the traditional children's party for the families of all the Embassy staff, both the UK and the local employees. In theory only mothers of toddlers were meant to attend and no fathers, but in practice everyone came to help or on some pretext—even the unmarried. Indeed, over the years the party had grown from "a big baby bash," as Melanie had inelegantly called it, to what could more aptly be described as an Embassy love-in. And as such it presented a perfect opportunity for another bomb threat or peculiar "incident." How could I help but be apprehensive? Things could so easily go wrong and we were very vulnerable.

I had considered cancelling the whole thing but I couldn't bring myself to do it, not only for the obvious reasons— the children's disappointment and the waste of all the planning and preparation—but also because of the publicity that would result; it would be as good as a public advertisement that the British Ambassador was running scared. Instead, I took every precaution I could think of, especially against any unwanted visitors sneaking into the Chancery among the party guests, and said a heartfelt prayer.

It was a lovely day, blue sky, sunshine and not very cold—too lovely; bitter weather might have cleared away our pickets. In fact, by the afternoon when Gaby and I arrived for the party, their lines had thinned somewhat; perhaps some of them had thought of a better way to celebrate Christmas. But too many of them remained and as the Rolls, pennant flying, drove past they raised an ironic cheer, shouted and waved to us. However, nobody threw anything and I wasn't aware of any personal animosity. They would trample on the flag gladly, from conviction or otherwise, but they hadn't taken to burning me in effigy—yet.

Gaby and I had purposely arrived a little late and the party was already under way. To judge by the shouts of merriment and the laughter and the general noise, it was swinging. Alex Stocker came bustling up to greet us. Our relations since Walter's party had been formal and strained but now, full of bonhomie, he was determined to be seasonably charitable. He overdid it a bit.

"There you are then, Mark," he said, after he had kissed Gaby and wished her a Happy Christmas. "Good. Good. We need H.E. to make the occasion." He didn't know how prophetic his words were to prove to be. "Come and make an arch for Oranges and Lemons."

"Delighted," I said, not be outdone.

And minutes later I was holding hands in the air with Sally Stocker, trying not to look down the too low clevage at her beautiful breasts, and asking myelf what, if anything, Alex was trying to prove.

"And here comes the chopper to chop-chop-chop off your head!"

The fair-haired child whom we had captured said, in an agonized bellow: "I wanna be on Mummy's side."

"That's my boy," Sally said lovingly and bent to kiss him; unexpectedly, at any rate to me, she was a devoted mum. "And so you shall, darling. You be an orange like Mummy. His Excellency is the lemon."

She gave me a wide, guileless smile and I switched on a polite, return smile. I would have liked to have asked her, as acidly as any lemon, if the unsuitable silk dress she was wearing was included in the bill for which she had given the boutique a dud cheque; but of course I couldn't. We started to sing again.

"Oranges and Lemons, say the bells of St. Clement's."

Sally had taken my hands and suddenly she squeezed them. Her voice grew soft. Her face had a lost look. For an unbelievable moment I thought she was trying to flirt with me. But it wasn't me she was dreaming about, or Alex either, as I learned later.

"And here comes the chopper," Sally sang, "to chop-chop-chop off your head."

I made my escape from Mrs. S. as soon as possible and slipped out the side door behind the tree. I wanted to check with the Duty and Security Officers that nothing suspicious or unusual had happened. Nothing had. A van had delivered some new Union Jacks to the pickets, presumably to impress the Christmas shoppers and the civil servants on their way home; the original "flags" were by now unrecognizable. But everything was peaceful.

By the time I returned to the party the "extra special tea" was in progress with Gaby in control. So I wandered around by myself, making idle conversation, pulling the occasional cracker, admiring a baby in arms and generally behaving like an MP at a garden fête. There was nothing else to do. Everything was very well organized and everyone but me seemed to have a job. I felt rather out of it.

Of course, at this point neither I nor anyone else had the faintest idea that I was to be the party's star turn.

After tea came the conjuror, who was very good indeed. Trick after trick got a rapturous reception. Even I relaxed and enjoyed his performance, until the finale. For this he coaxed from under the shelter of his arm a small reindeer. He was so convincing that, although the animal wasn't real, the illusion was complete. In fact I imagine the reindeer was made of some heavy material, painted and stretched on a trick frame. It made me think of the painted Union Jacks being scuffed by the pickets outside the Chancery and spoiled my pleasure.

As shrieks of laughter heralded the arrival of an irate Father Christmas looking for his stolen reindeer, I slipped away again to check with the Duty Officer and again he had nothing to report; indeed it was a quieter day than most. I told myself that I was being a fool. Nothing was going to happen. The party was nearly over and it had been a great success; nobody had tried to ruin it and nobody was going to try now. I had wasted a lot of worry; that was all.

I went back into the hall to watch Santa Claus distributing presents to a stream of children and I had to admire the way Alex was playing the part. He showed no signs of haste, he had a word and a smile for each child and he made gay quips at those awaiting their turn. But the piles of parcels around the base of the Christmas tree were dwindling with surprising speed. It was quite an act.

There were very few presents left when he picked up a

square box wrapped in gaily coloured paper and tied with scarlet ribbon.

"Here's a surprise," he cried. "Santa hasn't forgotten His Excellency. He has brought a present for the—the Ambassador." His voice faltered. "Sir—Sir Mark."

There was laughter and applause; the children alone received gifts from under the tree so this was a joke. Someone started to clap and everyone joined in.

But I didn't think it was a joke. As soon as I had heard Alex stutter I knew something was wrong. I moved towards him, blocking him from general view. His face was the colour of the cotton wool around his hood. His eyes, anguished, met mine. He held out the beribboned box at arm's length for me to take. The box ticked.

I wasn't aware of conscious thought. I tucked the box firmly under my arm and waved my thanks to the clapping children.

"Go on! Keep calm! Pretend nothing's happened," I hissed at Alex.

I was waving and backing towards the side of the tree, where there was only a handful of helpers. They smiled at me, innocently ignorant of what was happening, and I felt a wide smile stretched across my own face. I caught a glimpse of Gaby. The clapping subsided. I was at the door. As I closed it behind me I heard Alex calling out that Santa still had a few presents left; his voice was hoarse.

In the corridor I hesitated, clutching the box to my body; I was terrified of dropping it. I asked myself what I should do now. I didn't really know. If I had been at home I would have thrown it into a snowdrift in the garden, but outside the Chancery there would be office workers, shop assistants, bus queues, cars full of people, everyone going home at the end of a working day—even the damned pickets.

I had reached the lifts. I pressed the button and without any delay the pneumatic doors opened. I felt weak with gratitude. I got into the lift and the doors sighed shut behind me. In the enclosed space the ticking seemed to get louder and angrier. I leaned against the wall, sweating. My hands holding the box were damp. I didn't dare put it down. If I had I mightn't have had the guts to pick it up again.

In a strange way I felt light-headed. If the bloody thing exploded now I would be killed—but no one else. There would be no panic, no ghastly scene among the children. Not that I wanted to die. I thought of Gaby. Colette would be all right. But Gaby. I shut my eyes. I prayed incoherently for Gaby and myself.

The journey was interminable.

Eventually, however, the lift stopped and the doors opened. I stumbled out into the corridor. For an agnozing moment the box slithered between my fingers. Somehow I saved it.

Without thinking, I had pushed the top button in the lift so I had arrived at my own office floor, where there was always a guard on duty. I had completely forgotten about him. He was sitting at his desk with his feet up, drinking a cup of tea and reading. My sudden appearance startled him. He leapt to his feet, knocking over the tea, and came towards me.

"Get to hell out of the way!" I shouted wildly. "I've got a bomb in this box!"

He stopped as if I had hit him. His eyes widened. Then he drew his gun. He was afraid and likely to do anything. Maybe he thought I had gone off my head.

I fought to gain control of myself. I said icily: "Get back to your desk. Phone the Duty Officer. Tell him there's an unexploded bomb in my office. He must call the CFP but he must make them play it cool. We've still got a children's party downstairs. Hurry!"

"Sir!"

I walked through my secretary's office into my own room. I knew now exactly what I was going to do. I went into my private bathroom and put the box very carefully in the middle of the bath. I turned both taps on full. The ticking continued. I shielded myself with the door and waited.

The water pressure was poor and the bath filled slowly— very slowly, it seemed to me. When the water had reached the overflow and the box was completely submerged, I turned off the taps. I was almost out of the bathroom when the ticking stopped. I flung myself through the door, slamming it after me, and threw myself behind an armchair.

Nothing happened.

Nothing was going to happen.

Slowly I got to my feet. I was bruised and shaken. My shoulder hurt where I had hit it on the edge of the desk. I was trembling. I looked at my hands. They were multicoloured; the dyes from the Christmas wrapping had come off on my damp palms. But, although I was sweating, I was cold—and I wanted to be sick. I had to pull myself together. This reaction was absurd. There was no longer any danger. I was safe. And I couldn't be sick because I couldn't go into the bathroom. I grinned at the irony.

I went across the room and unlocked the cabinet where the liquor was kept. I poured myself three ounces of the finest quality Scotch which normally I reserved for my most high-powered visitors and drank it neat. That steadied me. I had put back the unwashed glass and was relocking the cabinet when the Security Officer put his head around the door.

"Are you all right, Sir Mark?"

"Quite all right, thank you."

"The police are on their way. The Commissioner's been informed and he'll be coming himself."

"Good, though I don't believe there's any danger. The box has stopped ticking but it hasn't exploded. It's soaking in the bath." I grimaced; my shoulder had given me a sudden twinge of pain. "I'm going downstairs for a while to get the party wound up. Nobody but nobody—and that includes you—is to go into the bathroom. Let the CFP handle it."

"Right, sir!"

I nodded. "I'll be back shortly."

I returned to the hall unobtrusively, by the door through which I had carried my obscene Christmas present. Alex had finished distributing the parcels from under the tree and everyone should have been singing carols, but somebody had had the sense to cut short the proceedings. I was in time to hear Gaby say in her usual quiet, unemotional voice:

"... His Excellency and I wish each one of you a very happy Christmas." She paused. She had seen me. She went on. "Perhaps you would all stand now so that before we go home we can sing our National Anthem together."

As those who were sitting on chairs or on the floor scrambled to their feet and the pianist began to play the opening bars of "God Save the Queen," I went to stand beside her. I took her hand and felt her fingers clutch desperately at me. I began to sing and presently she made a brave effort and joined me.

The moment the music ended the place became a babble of childish voices. The big doors at the end of the hall were thrown open. People began to leave. The party was over.

"Thank God!" Gaby said, and gave me a pathetic smile. "Oh, Mark!"

"It's all right, darling. Thank God, as you say. We've got a hell of a lot to be grateful for."

"Did it go off?"

"The bomb? No, but I think the danger's over. It's soaking in my bath at the moment. The CFP are going to deal with it. Alex told you?"

"Yes. But I knew somehow."

I nodded. "Where is Alex?"

"He said he was going to look for you."

"Well, I suggest we go up to his office. The CFP'll be swarming over mine." I glanced around the hall, which was emptying rapidly. Some of my staff seemed to be breaking up gossiping groups and shepherding the children; Alex must have passed on a warning. "There's nothing for us to do here."

When we got out of the lift we found Alex and the Security Officer clustered in the corridor with the Canadian Federal Police, who had just arrived. There were six CFP, headed by a sergeant, and they had with them a peculiar collection of equipment, presumably intended to help them defuse the bomb and give them some protection in case it went off. They began to carry the equipment into my office.

The sergeant asked a few pertinent questions. How big was the box? How long since it had stopped ticking? Was the box made of cardboard? But he didn't waste time. When he had got what information he could he ordered us to remove ourselves.

"We'll be in the Minister's office," I said, pointing down the corridor.

"Okay. You'll be safe there." He shook some Chiclets out of their packet and added them to the wadge of gum already in his mouth. "Okay!" he said again, impatiently.

And we went meekly along the corridor to Alex's rooms, Alex grumbling that the CFP were a rough lot, not like the old Mounties. Gaby and I were both too emotionally drained to respond or make unnecessary small talk. We sat and waited.

We didn't have to wait long.

The Commissioner of the Canadian Federal Police was a French Canadian, dark, dapper and, unlike his sergeant, excessively polite. He made an impressive entrance.

"Ah, Sir Mark," he said, "and Mr. Stocker. Your Ladyship." He bowed from the waist to Gaby. "I'm pleased to tell you—all is well."

My Security Officer was hovering behind him, trying to signal something to me. He looked angry.

"Thank you, Commissioner," I said. "I hope you didn't have any trouble?"

"No trouble, Sir Mark, not this time."

"Good."

"You're welcome. My men are highly trained and always at the service of the British Ambassador—as indeed we have demonstrated lately. This time, however, we were not needed." His mouth split into a wide grin. He brought from behind his back and placed on Alex's desk a large kitchen clock. "Here's your bomb, Sir Mark," he said. "Here's your present from Santa Claus."

There was a long moment of silence.

Then Alex exploded. "Damnable!" he said. "It was a damnable thing to do."

I said nothing. My feelings were a mixture of shame and hatred, shame that I had allowed myself to be tricked and hatred of whoever had tricked me. I had made a fool of myself, a laughing-stock. I swallowed my bile.

"It's only my idea, mind you, Sir Mark," the Commissioner was saying, "but I don't think your enemy has done as good as he hoped. I think perhaps you were meant to throw yourself heroically on the—bomb in front of all your staff and their families. There would have been a big panic and, afterwards, you would have appeared still foolisher." He shook his head. "Very bad for the image."

I gave him a hard look; he was more astute than I had thought. "Oh, we mustn't read too much into a sick joke, Commissioner," I said and began to get to my feet. "I'm sorry that we had to bother you."

But the Commissioner hadn't finished. "One moment, please, Sir Mark," he said.

His timing was excellent. Almost immediately there was a rap on the door, which swung inwards allowing my Security Officer to enter. A hand, the extension of an arm in regulation CFP uniform, closed the door behind him. His own hands were occupied.

He was carrying a desk blotter which he had laid carefully in front of me. On it was a soggy bit of card covered with writing. The Commissioner passed me a magnifying-glass and I peered through it. Alex was breathing down my neck. I felt absurd; Sherlock Holmes was not my line.

"You may touch it if you like," the Commissioner said. "No prints."

"What is it?" Alex asked. "Where did it come from?"

"It was in the box containing the clock." The Commissioner addressed himself to me. "As to what it is—" he shrugged—"you British have enemies, I regret."

"It's sad they should be Canadians," Gaby said suddenly, speaking in French. "We wish your country well, Commissioner."

"I believe you, madame," he said seriously. "Alas, all my fellow countrymen do not agree with me."

His second statement was certainly true. I stared at the card on the blotter. It had been damaged by the bath water and the words were blurred, some of them indecipherable. But there was no doubt about their meaning. The message couldn't have been clearer. The Arctic belonged to Canadians to hand on to their children and their children's children. It was their birthright. British children must not be allowed to reap the benefits that should belong to Canadians.

The clock was a warning; it could have been a bomb. Next time it might be.

Feeling cold and slightly sick, I said: "You're quite right, Commissioner, we do have enemies. But this one's obviously a crank. The best thing's to ignore the whole affair."

"We can't just leave it at that," Alex objected.

"We'll make some enquiries about how the parcel could have been put under the Christmas Tree," I said, "and tighten up security in the Chancery. But we needn't worry the Commissioner any more. I'm extremely grateful to you, Commissioner."

"You're welcome, Your Excellency," he said formally.

He stood up; he was ready to go now. I would have loved to have known what he really thought—about the bomb outside the Residence, the shooting at Edgar King's lot, the bomb scare yesterday at the Chancery and this latest incident. We had been keeping his men busy.

As if he had read my thoughts he said: "I wish you all a Merry Christmas and a New Year free from any more unpleasant excitements." He shook hands with each of us and bowed himself out.

I sighed with relief as the door shut behind him. I had had enough. So, I was to discover, had Gaby.

But we weren't quite finished yet. The Security Officer, full of apologies, said there was a gaggle of reports and a couple of camera men downstairs. They refused to go away. The Press Officer, for the sake of good relations, had asked them to wait in the hall—what did I want to do about them?

"I don't want to do anything about them," I said brusquely. They were the last straw. "When we've gone give them the bare bones. No comment. And play it down."

"Yes, Sir Mark," he said.

The newsmen, however, were not to be thwarted so easily. They clustered around Gaby and myself as we tried to leave, firing questions and clicking cameras. There were more of them than one would have expected; obviously they had had a tip-off. They already knew the broad outlines of what had happened and had some version of the message enclosed with the alarm clock. Now they wanted to know precisely what I'd done and precisely what I'd felt. And I'd see them to hell before I told them.

No comment!

The questions came thicker, not all of them sympathetic; I'd made a fool of myself and I was fair game. There were one or two jeering remarks, some amusement at my expense, a crack about Carmine. It was my own fault. I should have made a short statement; it wouldn't have satisfied them but it wouldn't have riled them either. It was too late now. I had handled the situation badly.

No comment!

We had almost reached the Rolls. The chauffeur was holding the door open for us. Somebody shouted: "No comment's not much of a Christmas present for us. Can't you think of anything better to say?"

"Yes! I can!"

I was more surprised than anyone else. Gaby had pulled her arm away from me and had turned to face them. There were two spots of colour high up on the cheekbones of her pale face and her eyes were very bright. Her voice shook a little.

"What would you have done? Ask yourself that, each one of you. If you had been in my husband's place, what would *you* have done?"

There was a moment of shocked silence. And a roar of laughter as somebody said: "I'd have pissed in my pants." But this was followed at once by cries of "Good for you, Lady Lowrey," and "Well done, Lady Lowrey," and a chorus of "Merry Christmas." They weren't against us any more.

But Gaby hadn't waited for their response. She had turned her back on them and was getting into the car. The chauffeur closed the door behind us and the Rolls drew away from the kerb. She sat deep in her corner so they wouldn't see the tears running down her cheeks. She tried to smile at me. I've never seen her look more beautiful.

"Thank you, darling," I said. "Thank you." And I took her in my arms. If the pickets were still parading in front of the Chancery, treading the Union Jacks into the slush and mouthing their slogans, I didn't notice them. Britain could look after herself for a while.

CHAPTER 8

December 24

ABOUT A MONTH ago Gaby and I had decided to give a reception on Christmas Eve and, even if we had wished, there was no question of cancelling it at the last minute. We were expecting about a hundred guests.

I wasn't looking forward to shaking a hundred arriving hands and a hundred departing hands. I had hit my right shoulder on the desk yesterday when the supposed bomb stopped ticking and I dived for safety. I hadn't broken anything but the bone was badly bruised and the whole arm ached. I ought to have had it in a sling, which of course was impossible. I could scarcely appear as a wounded hero.

The funny thing was that by chance I *was* something of a hero. Because there had happened to be a dearth of hard news the media, both last night and today, had made much of the incident at the Embassy party. Moreover, thanks to Gaby, they had been exceedingly kind to me. They had taken to heart her pertinent question—what would you have done? And since nobody had been able to come up with a better answer than I had, nobody had been in any position to mock me.

On the contrary, the original scenario had come badly unstuck. Instead of becoming a figure of fun I had earned myself a lot of Brownie points. Woods-Dawson was going to be pleased. But personally I wanted to forget the whole thing; even thinking of it made me feel sick.

I sighed. It was a quarter to eight, high time I went downstairs. Our guests would soon be arriving. I found Gaby and Melanie already in the drawing-room.

Melanie was saying: ". . . room look terribly attractive."

"Thank you," Gaby said. "I think they're worth the effort."

She was referring to the strings of Christmas cards from all over the world that hung in festoons on the walls. They and a dozen poinsettias were the only decorations. (There was no tree to remind us of yesterday.) And the room was attractive.

But that Melanie should say so was surprising; she wasn't apt to pay Gaby compliments. She must be in a mellow mood, I thought; with luck it might last over Christmas. I couldn't keep up with my sister's moods lately. For instance, last night she had been extraordinarily understanding about the clock-bomb and had insisted on helping Gaby to strap my shoulder. But the night before she had delivered a tirade when I announced that John Coller could no longer be *persona grata* to the Lowreys, so that I had been forced to tell her, against Woods-Dawson's express orders, that Coller was in the Central Intelligence Agency and only then had she reluctantly agreed to be distant if we happened to meet him somewhere. Gaby had a theory that Melanie had broken with her Oxford professor and hence her moods. Maybe Gaby was right. It was too much to hope that this could be a final parting . . .

"Mark!"

"Darling, I'm sorry. What did you say?"

"Melanie asked you if you'd taken any precautions against gatecrashers."

"Oh—yes, in a mild way."

"You're not expecting any excitement tonight then?"

"My dear Melanie, I never expect any excitement. At any rate not the sort that happens," I said bitterly.

"I'm praying for a quiet, dull party," Gaby said.

Melanie laughed. "I think I heard the bell. Let's hope old Walter isn't the first arrival as usual."

I should have been surprised if he had been; Walter had once been Chief of Protocol and knew the difference be-

tween dining privately with the Lowreys and a formal
affair. In fact the first to arrive, at five minutes to the
hour, were a few of the Embassy staff and their wives
whose turn it was to help entertain the guests. It was part
of the job and good practice for the juniors, though most
of them would have preferred to be at home decorating
their own trees and wrapping up their children's presents.
We stood around, sipping our drinks and making slightly
stilted conversation.

It was a quarter of an hour before the next people came
but after that there was a steady flow. General and Mrs. A.,
the Right Honourable John and Mrs. B., Dr. and Mrs. C.,
Monsieur et Madame E, His Excellency—etc., etc. The
houseman announced the names; Gaby and I shook hands;
we exchanged a few words; the guests passed on to drink
and chat—one hoped to enjoy themselves. They had already
handed in their invitation cards and signed the visitors' book;
my chauffeur, in the role of major-domo, was in charge of
that part of the proceedings. The knack was for Gaby and
myself to welcome each guest as if he or she was really
important to us or particularly welcome for some reason. It
wasn't always easy.

A rather surly Head of Division in External Affairs was
followed by Mr. and Mrs. Alex Stocker, the Norwegian
Ambassador and his lady, and a couple whom we were very
pleased to see, Paul and Lucille Brill, to whom we had sent
an invitation with a personal note attached the day after the
Kings' snowmobiling party.

"How nice of you to come," Gaby said warmly.

"Our pleasure," Paul Brill said, "and we're glad to be
able to offer you our sympathy for what happened yesterday.
To plant a psuedo-bomb under a children's Christmas tree
was a dreadful thing to do."

"Thank you," we said together.

"The CFP have no idea who—" Paul was tentative.

"None," I said.

"Someone who dislikes the Carmine Project, according
to the newscasters," he said.

"The same someone who knows damn all about it," I
snapped.

Paul nodded. "The U.S. Ambassador got a similar parcel, I hear, but his staff dealt with it."

"Really?" Lucille broke the tension. "I think your husband was wonderful," she said to Gaby.

"So do I," Gaby agreed, "but I always do."

We laughed politely and Paul mentioned the President's skating party on New Year's Day. We talked about it until the next guests were announced. The Brills promised to look out for us at the Palace. I thought about them as I greeted the new arrivals. Lucille had been very friendly, but Paul—I didn't know. I had a distinct impression that he had tossed his Carmine remark at me deliberately, to see my reaction; and I'd certainly reacted.

There was a burst of guests and then the houseman intoned: "Mr. and Mrs. Edgar King."

I braced myself. I expected to have to parry a spate of personal questions. Heather had telephoned first thing this morning and kept Gaby for more than twenty minutes demanding every detail of what had happened at the Embassy party. But now she didn't mention the subject.

And Edgar referred to it only obliquely, by emphasizing how glad he was that Gaby and I were both fine. In return Gaby said how pleased we were that Edgar himself was well again; the polite fiction was that some bug had caused him to pass out after his snowmobiling efforts last Saturday. He grinned at us cheerfully and pumped my hand until the pain in my shoulder became acute. I must have shown it because he looked at me anxiously.

"You're sure you're okay, Mark?"

"Yes, of course."

"You're as pale as—"

"Just tired, that's all."

In fact I was wondering how much more handshaking I could take. It was quarter past nine. The room was full. Almost everyone had come by now and some had left. Perhaps I could swallow another codeine before the farewells began in earnest.

I endured the half-dozen guests who had followed the Kings and said, to Gaby: "Would you mind if I circulated for a while? My shoulder needs a rest."

"Of course not, darling. There can't be many more arrivals."

"Thank God!"

Gaby laughed. "Mark, you might rescue the Israeli Ambassador. From his frozen face I'd guess Melanie's lecturing him on his country's recent misbehaviour to the States."

"Poor man! I will."

But our brief conversation had given the houseman time to announce Walter Eland. I offered him my left hand. Walter was full of apologies and didn't comment. He apologized for being late and he apologized for having forgotten to bring his invitation card.

"I don't think your chaps would've let me in if they hadn't recognized me," he said.

"I'm sure they would," I said, "but the houseman would've kept an eye on you."

Walter pulled at his moustache. "I don't blame you. You've been leading a dangerous life lately, haven't you?"

"I'm certainly tired of sick jokes."

"Is that all they are?"

"Well, nobody's going to assassinate me, if that's what you're implying," I said. "As an individual I'm of no importance and as H.E. I'd be replaced at once. What's more, the new Ambassador would profit enormously from my martyrdom."

"Which I find a very comforting thought," Gaby said drily.

"My dear Gaby!" Walter was embarrassed.

"Come and have a drink," I said. "I'm going to desert my post for a few minutes."

"Yes," he said. "I'd like a word with you."

He avoided looking at me and I wondered what was amiss. We strolled over to the bar together. Walter asked for a rye and ginger and I settled for a short, strong Scotch; I wouldn't be able to leave Gaby for the length of a leisurely drink and I needed something to dull the pain in my shoulder.

"Mark," Walter said tentatively.

"Yes," I said, and the thought that he was going to ask me for Melanie's hand in marriage strayed absurdly across my mind; I grinned at it.

"It's not in the least humourous."

"I'm sorry. Perhaps you'd tell me."

"I was visiting an aunt of mine earlier this evening." Walter had innumerable aunts. "She's very pro-British, incidentally. Her first husband was a Scot. She told me she had it on excellent authority that the Carmine Project isn't exactly what it appears to be."

"She watches too much television—people like Senator Portman," I said abrasively, remembering too late that it was at Walter's party I had had my unfortunate conversation with the Senator.

"No. She's not a fool." Walter turned away in exasperation as a couple came up to say goodbye to me. "You interrupted me before I could make my point," he said. "She wasn't just repeating an idle rumour started by that ass Portman. I can't tell you her source but he's someone in the Opposition Front Bench, and he maintains that the Carmine bases are being built in such a way as to be adaptable for military purposes."

"That's absolute nonsense," I said. But it was a repetition of the potentially explosive story that Gavin Brown had heard in Montreal. I didn't know what to make of it.

"Precisely what my aunt said. However, after the Christmas recess he intends to table a question in the House. I thought you should be warned, Mark."

"Yes. Thank you, Walter. I'm grateful, though God knows what can be done about it. And I'm sorry I maligned your aunt."

"Forget it—and forget I ever mentioned the matter, will you?"

"Of course."

Hoping that Woods-Dawson might have some bright idea about this new line in Carmine rumours, I collected another drink and mingled with my guests. Several of them were preparing to leave, including Paul and Lucille Brill. I wished them goodbye and a Happy Christmas. Walter, I was amused to notice, had made straight for Melanie; the Israeli Ambassador had already escaped and she was chatting with the Stockers. I avoided Heather King and the American Cultural

Attaché. It was time I returned to Gaby. I glanced towards the door to see how she was getting on by herself—and froze.

She was talking to John Coller.

What in hell's name was John Coller doing in my house, at my party? We hadn't met him until last week, long after the invitations had been sent out, and he certainly hadn't been invited since; the only people who had were the Brills. But the idea that he would have gate-crashed was ludicrous; according to Woods-Dawson he should have been as eager to avoid me as I was to avoid him. Yet here he was standing, uninvited, in my drawing-room.

Beside him was a girl in a shocking pink trouser suit. She was small and slender with long black hair, very attractive. I had never seen her before and had no idea who she was. I assumed she had come with Coller.

However, there was some confusion. Coller and the unknown girl were arriving. The Brills were leaving; I noticed that they responded to Coller's greetings very distantly. And in the background, still waiting to be announced, hovered one of my neighbors, a retired General. I hurried over to them.

"Hullo, Mark, and a Merry Christmas to you."

Coller shook my hand. It was the first time that he had addressed me so familiarly. Even after we had been shot at and had been lying in the snow together under the trees he had added the handle to my name or called me Ambassador. Now, it seemed, we were chums.

"I'm sorry I'm so late but I had to go and have a drink with old Harry and it was difficult to get away."

I mumbled something. I hadn't a clue who old Harry was; I never did find out so he can't have been important. I saw Paul Brill turn in the doorway and give me an odd look—or I imagined it. I wondered suddenly if he knew that John Coller was in the CIA.

Gaby was introducing me to the unknown girl, who turned out to be the General's married daughter. So Coller couldn't be blamed for bringing the girl after all. He removed himself tactfully as the General began to explain how his wife had been unable to drag herself away from her grandchildren. I watched him collect a drink and then make a bee-line for Melanie. Perhaps he considered it his duty to make a point of greeting my sister, but I wished he hadn't.

I excused myself to the General and his daughter and went into the hall. I wanted to know why Coller, uninvited, had been admitted so casually. Unlike Walter, he had never been to the Residence before and was unknown to my chauffeur and my houseman. Woods-Dawson's men seemed to have fallen down.

I found them conferring together or maybe they were relieving their boredom by having a chat. But they leaped towards me.

"Everything all right, Sir Mark?"

"The General vouched for the girl, Sir Mark. He said she was—"

"Forget her," I said. "What about Mr. John Coller?"

"The American? He had a card, Sir Mark."

"Let me see it."

All our invitation cards had been engraved in the UK. They were thick, expensive and beautifully embossed. This made them difficult to duplicate. As an additional precaution on this occasion, because a large party is always vulnerable to gate-crashers, Gaby had herself written in the guests' names. There was nothing we could do if people forgot to bring their cards, of course, but in theory the major-domo should have been able to check the alphabetical guest list while the suspect characters signed the book; in practice this wasn't always possible. But we had had no trouble. And anyway it didn't apply to Coller. He had received an invitation card which he had brought with him.

I held it in my hand and looked at it. There was no doubt that it was genuine. Moreover I knew now why he had come—or I assumed I did.

On the back of his card, in the same handwriting as the Mr. John Coller on the other side—Gaby's handwriting—was written: "Please do come. Mark."

It wasn't necessary to ask Gaby if she had sent Coller an invitation but I did all the same. She lifted her head, looked down her long nose at me and said: "No!" I whispered that I would explain later. A stream of departing guests was approaching.

While I uttered Christmas wishes, kissed cheeks, shook hands and tried to nurse my shoulder I thought about John Coller—if thinking isn't too flattering a word to apply to the scattered impressions which crossed my mind. I couldn't decide whether to ignore his uninvitedness or to tell him that he had been tricked. I'm ashamed to admit that the latter would have given me some satisfaction—Woods-Dawson had spoken enviously of him being one of CIA's brightest boys—but it occurred to me that he might have known it was a trick and had come, nevertheless, to find out why anybody had bothered to deceive him.

This was the real mystery, because nothing untoward had happened the whole evening. In fact it had been the quiet, dull party for which Gaby had said she was praying.

And, thank God, it was almost over.

There were so few guests remaining that they were co-agulating into one group. I yearned for them all to go. The Kings were breaking away. Heather said goodbye to Melanie and to Coller, who was still beside my sister. Edgar kissed Melanie and rudely, so it seemed to me, turned his back on Coller. I assumed he was drunk again but he wasn't. When he came to say goodbye to Gaby and myself he was warm and friendly and fully in control; he must have snubbed Coller on purpose.

Goodbye. Goodbye and a Merry Christmas.

Lovely party. Thank you so very much.

Thank you for coming. Goodbye. Happy Christmas.

Happy Christmas. Merry Christmas. Thank you. Goodbye.

And I shook the last departing hand. It belonged to John Coller. He had stayed until the bitter end but we can't have exchanged more than a dozen words. He must have been as mystified as I was as to what he had been doing at the British Residence, or I hoped he was.

Melanie had gone to bed and Gaby and I were getting ready to go to Midnight Mass when the houseman said I was wanted on the telephone.

"Who is it? Manchester?"

"No, Sir Mark. I don't know who it is. He wouldn't give his name."

"What?"

He vetted all my calls at the Residence so I was never bothered by reporters or importunate callers or cranks. What, then, was so different about this no-name?

"He's the man you told me about, sir, the one who tele-phoned the night our post-box was blown up, or so he says. And he's very insistent. Will you speak to him?"

"Good God, I'd forgotten all about that chap. Yes, I'll speak to him but stall him a minute. I must tape it."

I hurried down to the study, switched on the recorder and lifted the receiver. I could hear him breathing. There was a click as the houseman replaced the phone.

"Good evening," I said. "This is the British Ambassador, Sir Mark Lowrey."

He skipped all greetings. "Last time I brought you a warning. This time I bring you good tidings."

"The Angel Gabriel?" I murmured; I didn't intend him to hear.

"What was that?"

It was pure Anglo-Saxon. Nobody whose native tongue wasn't English could have given the words that precise intonation. And somewhere in my memory they rang a faint bell.

"What is it?" I asked. "What is your good news?"

"It's all over. Finished. You don't have to worry no more, Your Excellency." His French accent was back thicker than before. "I'm your—your friend. I wanted you to know so that you could enjoy your Christmas."

"What is finished?"

"Your—your troubles. There won't be no more sick jokes, no more shootings or bombings or traps for your sister. Nothing like that. No more personal attacks. They're fin-ished, I tell you. No more. They've got what they wanted from you."

I caught my breath. The "shootings and bombings" he could have read about in the paper or heard on the news. But how did he know about Melanie? He must have been referring to the incident in *The Canada Goose*, and he could only have known about that if he himself was incriminated. He wasn't a crank.

"Who are you?" I said. "Can I help you? Are you in some trouble? I'll help you if I can."

"No. There's no need. Don't you understand? It's all over. Your party tonight was the end. The Commies have got what they wanted and there's nothing you can do about it. So have a happy Christmas. Goodbye."

He had rung off. Slowly I put down the receiver and switched on the tape. I heard it through twice before Gaby came to tell me that it was time we left for the Cathedral. I still couldn't find any tidings of great joy in the message or any reason why I should now be able to enjoy Christmas. On the contrary I felt like a condemned man before a hearty breakfast.

PART TWO

New Year

CHAPTER 1

January 1

IT WAS NEW YEAR'S DAY. Christmas had come and gone. As my anonymous telephone caller had predicted, there had been no more "shootings or bombings," no more inexplicable incidents and no more acts or threats of violence that concerned me personally. Nevertheless no one could say that there had been many signs of peace and goodwill around either.

Over the holiday a wave of anti-British, anti-American feeling had spread right across the country. No major city had been without its pickets and its protest rallies. On Boxing Day about 1500 people had crowded into Toronto's Nathan Phillips Square to hear charges that Britain was "taking over" the Arctic. A rally in the Calgary Stampede grounds against British and American economic domination of Canada had ended in a near riot. And students in Vancouver, demonstrating daily in opposition to the non-existent American presence in the North, had become a source of civic disruption. But perhaps most unpleasant was the small Nova Scotian, who had won national fame as the boy on the poster that read: "I hate the Brits and the Yanks 'cos they're misusing my Northland."

I thrust these unhappy thoughts to the back of my mind. I had better things to think of tonight. We were on our way to the President's skating party at Rideau Palace—supposedly the highlight of the Ottawa Christmas season—and I was rather looking forward to it, not least because of seeing Paul Brill again.

And better than their promise, the Brills were actually waiting for us. With them was Lucille's brother, a fat but engaging lawyer from Quebec City, who explained that as he too was a stranger to Ottawa he hoped he might have the honour of escorting Mademoiselle Lowrey. Melanie, half asleep after a hard day's skiing with the Stockers—she seemed to spend most of her time with Sally Stocker—couldn't help but be charmed.

"I'm an excellent skater, if you'll permit me to boast," the little lawyer said. "Indeed, so are Lucille and Paul. On this occasion we are all set to support—if necessary literally—the British Ambassador and his ladies."

"After that fair speech," Paul said, "Gabrielle and Melanie will probably turn out to be ex-European champions. And your face, Jean-Pierre, will be very red."

"Not at all," Gaby said. "I'm afraid none of us are very good at it."

"But you do skate, Mark?" Paul sounded almost anxious. "That's the important thing."

"Obviously, *chéri,*" Lucille said soothingly. "They wouldn't have come equipped otherwise. Now let's get ready and go along to the lake. I'm told they're serving hot punch there. We can have some refreshment before we go on the ice."

The thought, a faint suspicion that we were being organized and that the Brills' friendliness, while genuine, contained some other purpose, crossed my mind. It was born of Paul's seeming nervousnes; he was distrait and more than once looked at his watch. I didn't like to question him. There could have been a hundred reasons, none of them my business. Besides, Lucille and her brother were keeping us entertained.

And soon I was really enjoying myself. With Lucille's help I found my sense of rhythm and we went swinging over the ice to the music which came from loud-speakers hidden in the frost-covered trees. The exercise, the crisp air, the general gaiety and the warmth of the toddy in my

stomach gave me a wonderful sense of well-being which I
hadn't had for weeks.

I was sorry when, at a pause in the music, Lucille drifted
me across to Gaby and Paul, who were skating decorously
near the bank. And I was abashed when Lucille, laughing
at my thanks, said I was a competent skater but not very
adventurous. I had felt terrific.

"I thought I did rather well," I said.

"You were splendid, darling," Gaby said. "I was impressed at any rate." She grinned at me.

Paul looked at his watch yet again. "Come and have a
spin with me," he said.

"Love to," I agreed with alacrity.

I wouldn't have been so enthusiastic had I known that
my evening was about to be ruined. But, happily ignorant,
I struck out beside Paul. He didn't waste much time. Almost
at once he said: "Mark, I have an invitation for you. The
President would be pleased if you would skate with him."

I took a gulp of icy air that hurt my chest. "I should be
honoured."

"Good. Let's go, then. We'll find him at the far end of
the lake."

And find him we did, giving, to my dismay, an exhibition
of virtuoso skating before an admiring group. I wondered
what I had let myself in for. If I was expected to take part
in this display the results were going to be at best funny
and at worst disastrous. In the event I needn't have worried.
The President must have caught sight of Paul because, in-
scribing an arc, he came to a halt and gave a mocking bow
to the applauding audience. The entertainment was over.
The watchers dispersed and the President skated across to
where we waited. Paul presented me.

"I hope, *Excellence,* that you don't expect me to emulate
you," I said.

"No, no, Sir Mark." He smiled; he had big white teeth
like a film star's. "We shall go softly, you and I, so that we
can talk."

He offered me his hands and we moved over the ice
together slowly, making a wide circle. Two security men

skated behind and another couple in front to our left, but nobody could hear what was said. This was indeed a private audience, something to impress Woods-Dawson and a nice sweetener in my next ambassadorial report. But most important it was an opportunity to make some real contact with this man, for whom I had had an enormous respect ever since I had studied Woods-Dawson's file on him. I had to make the most of it.

"We don't have much time, Sir Mark, so I won't squander it being diplomatic." The President who was completely bilingual spoke in French.

I took it as a compliment. I said: *"Je suis á votre service, Excellence."*

"First I want to say how much I regret recent Canadian hostility towards the British and the Americans. It's not the policy of my government to condone outrages against the persons and property of foreign representatives."

I didn't like his linking the British and the Americans so closely, or his emphasis on the word 'foreign.' I said: "Thank you, *Excellence,* on behalf of the British."

"Such outrages come in waves, as you're aware, Sir Mark, often over a period of public holiday. This little lot will soon be over. We're rounding up some of the culpits. Not the real culpits, of course—they're much too clever— but those they use."

I looked sideways and down at the President; he was a head shorter than I was, a thick-set man, over seventy, older than my father. He had dark skin, high cheekbones, a prominent nose and large, sad, brown eyes; it was said that he had Indian blood. At the moment I could only see the top of his knitted cap, with its absurd bobble. That told me nothing.

When the President next spoke it was in English. "I would like, Sir Mark, to ask you about the Carmine Project," he said.

I wasn't unduly surprised. I said: "I understand, *Excellence,* that it's making better progress than was expected."

"Good, Sir Mark. Very good! But do you also understand that to Canadians it's becoming—*merde, une énorme merde?*"

"Yes. A—a five-letter word in French. I realize that." I paused. Was it Clausewitz who said attack was the best defence—or Hannibal? One day I was going to read some military history; the subject had always fascinated me. *"Excellence,* may I speak frankly? May I remind you that when agreement on the Carmine Project was reached it was you, on behalf of Canada, who signed the public—and the private—clauses, so you know what an enormous amount in material terms Canada stands to gain. Moreover, if our enemies—our mutual enemies—succeed in destroying what was devised and undertaken by Her Majesty's Government as a demonstration of continued goodwill to the people of Canada, then they may succeed in destroying not only these material advantages but also the bond between our countries. With respect, *Excellence,* I believe that would be an even greater disaster for Canada than for the United Kingdom."

"And what of the Americans, Sir Mark? What have they got to lose or gain?"

"Nothing whatsoever, *Excellence*. They're providing a minute proportion of the personnel and equipment—preference is always given to Canadian or British—but that is all. Any other suggestion is a mere *canard."*

For a full minute we skated in silence. My ankles were beginning to ache at the unaccustomed exercise. I envied the old President his stamina. I wanted a rest but didn't dare suggest it. I waited for him to speak.

At last he said: "They say of us Canadians that all we want is *un bon boss et un job steady.* But it's not true, Sir Mark, not any more. We're prepared to sell our *potage* for a mess of birthright."

I chose my words carefully. "Perhaps that mightn't be a bad bargain. It's for Canada to decide. But we're afraid for her, *Excellence,* lest she sign away her birthright with the *potage."*

"So am I," he said. "So am I. That's why I need to know about your sister, Dr. Melanie Lowrey."

"My sister? Mel—"

I was so surprised that I stopped skating. One foot caught up with the other and I pecked at the ice. I would have fallen but the President saved me. We came to an undignified stop with a flurry of arms and legs; the shoulder which I had hurt during the children's party gave an unpleasant twinge and I winced. The damned old man was grinning broadly.

"It's not fair, Sir Mark, is it? I've taken advantage of you. When you should be preparing diplomatic answers you have to worry about not taking a prat fall. But I don't want diplomatic answers, I want the truth. And your body betrays only the truth."

"I have no cause to lie, *Excellence,* certainly not about my sister."

"She's a very clever woman, eh?"

"I suppose so. She's a professor of political science at Oxford. She has written two or three books. She lectures and appears on television."

He made a throwaway gesture. "Sir Mark, I know all that. I don't doubt that she's clever in theory—but in practice? Does she make you a good go-between with Washington?"

I stared into his heavy-lidded eyes. His trenched face was expressionless. *"Excellence,* you have been misinformed," I said slowly. "My sister's in Ottawa on a private visit. She has no connection—go-between or otherwise—with Her Majesty's Government or the Government of the United States. Anything you have heard to the contrary is completely unfounded."

He smiled at me without humour. "That's the kind of unequivocal statement that comes to haunt politicians and diplomats." He shook his head mournfully.

I wasn't sure if this signified reproach or disbelief or what. I had to convince him. "It's the truth," I said.

"Before she came to Ottawa she was in Washington. She visited the State Department and the CIA?"

"She was in Washington, yes. At some academic conference. As far as I know she never went near the State Department or the Agency."

"With Mr. John Coller, her old and close friend?"

'No. She didn't know Coller then. She's not an old friend of his. That was a rumour started by an Ottawa newspaper that erroneously reported her being at the National Arts

Centre Ball with John Coller when, in fact, she was with somebody else—Mr. Walter Eland of External Affairs."

"Well, if not old, will you agree to the word 'close?' Dr. Lowrey and Mr. Coller are close friends, are they not?"

"No, *Excellence,* they are not. They haven't met half a dozen times."

"Did you know, Sir Marks, that John Coller worked for the Central Intelligence Agency?"

I hesitated. Woods-Dawson had been insistent that Coller's cover shouldn't be endangered. He would go around the bend at the thought of my blowing it to the President of Canada. But some instinct urged me not to prevaricate. I heard myself saying: "Yes, I was informed of that quite recently. And, *Excellence,* once I knew, there was no longer any possibility that my family's slight social acquaintance with him could ripen into friendship. I wouldn't risk the possibility of giving offence to you or your government."

The President didn't answer. Instead he held out his hands to me. "Let's skate again. It's cold standing here on the ice. At my age the blood runs thin."

Reluctantly I accepted his royal command, and we began to move across the frozen lake. The security men who had been skating in a respectful circle around us took up their former positions fore and aft. From the loudspeakers in the trees came the strains of the perennially popular "Hello, Dolly." I noticed that Paul Brill had reappeared and guessed that my meeting with the President was coming to an end.

"Sir, Mark, please don't be offended if I say that I believe you've not lied to me. Nevertheless, what you've told me about your sister is not the truth. She is John Coller's mistress."

"His mistress?" I would have laughed if I hadn't had to make an effort to keep the rhythm of the skating.

"Yes. Melanie Lowrey and John Coller are lovers," he said sadly. "Every day she goes to meet him in her little yellow car. Sometimes she goes to his apartment. Sometimes they ski together in the Gatineau. He has a winterized cottage near Lake—"

"Excellence!" I interrupted. "My sister doesn't have a car in Ottawa, yellow or otherwise."

"It is an Austin America, the new model, rented for her use by the American Embassy. Paul will give you the licence number and other details."

I didn't know what to say. I couldn't go on reiterating that he was wrong, wrong, wrong. The situation was ridiculous. I was as sure as I could be that he wasn't deliberately lying to me and he had accepted that I wasn't lying to him. But neither of us believed a word the other said!

A man came hurrying from the direction of the Palace. He stood on the edge of the bank and signalled to the President and to Paul. They both waved an acknowledgement.

"That was one of my aides," the President said. "I've been expecting some important documents. It seems they've come so I must leave you. Later on tonight, when you're ready to go home, Paul will give you a small packet. Its contents will substantiate all I've told you. You'll of course take what action you think best, Sir Mark, but please do nothing hasty. We'll meet again soon, I think. *Au revoir.*"

A hand in the small of my back and a gentle but powerful thrust sent me skimming over the ice towards Paul, faster than I would have chosen. I barely had time to throw a goodbye over my shoulder, but what of it? At the moment I didn't care a damn about protocol. I concentrated on coming to a dignified stop before I reached Paul Brill.

"I'd like to rejoin my wife now," I said.

"Of course." He gave me a tentative smile. "She's having coffee by the bonfire. Melanie's still skating."

"Perhaps you'd be good enough to ask her to join us too—if your agent has finished questioning her."

"Agent? Oh no, I assure you. Jean-Pierre's Lucille's brother and he's a lawyer. He's interested in Quebec politics but not in international affairs. He knows nothing about this business—nothing at all."

"But you do? You have your President's confidence?"

"Yes."

"So you know what we've been talking about and what's in this packet you're going to give me later on?"

"Yes. And I am to say that when you've seen the contents yourself if there's anything you want to ask or anything I can do, I'm at your disposal."

"You're too kind."

He ignored my sarcasm. "These are difficult times, for all of us."

His remark could have meant a lot or nothing. "There's one thing you could tell me now," I said. "Where's my sister meant to be keeping this little yellow car of hers?"

He answered without a second's hesitation. "At the home of your Minister, Alex Stocker."

I was thankful I wasn't still skating with the President. He would have felt the shock go through my body. Until then I hadn't given the slightest credence to his story of a relationship between Melanie and John Coller, political or otherwise. I had immediately assumed that it was another piece of communist trickery, sustained by rumours and circumstantial evidence, which Melanie and I together would be easily able to refute—now that we had a chance to do so. I didn't think the communists had expected that we should ever have such a chance.

But, at the mention of Alex Stocker, a spasm of doubt shook me. It was instinctive and irrational—and it sapped my confidence. Paul Brill had been so positive.

I wiped the back of my mitten across my face as if to clear my mind. We had reached the more populated part of the lake and I could see the bonfire blazing spectacularly in the snow with a small crowd around it; Gaby would be among them. And on the ice Jean-Pierre was trying without much success, to teach Melanie to dance. I thought how much I would have liked to collect Gaby and Melanie and inform Paul Brill that we were leaving. But I could recognize the impossible. The niceties had to be observed—unless, of course, I wanted to encourage comment; the more favoured members of the Press would certainly be present on this social occasion. And the evening had to be endured.

I endured it, though it wasn't easy. I chatted to friends and acquaintances; I drank champagne; I filled my plate from the opulent buffet and ate a reasonable amount; I watched the President appear, greet a few privileged guests and disappear; I avoided Lucille Brill and her brother, Jean-Pierre. Paul Brill was nowhere to be seen. Doubtless he was somewhere with the President discussing my reactions to the preposterous story I had just been told. The evening dragged on.

But eventually the party ended and Paul reappeared to wish us good-night and to give me a brown manilla envelope, stuffed to its capacity. I thanked him and wished him a happy New Year. I offered him my hand. If he couldn't be my friend I didn't want him as an enemy; he carried too much clout.

"I hope sincerely that it'll be a happy New Year for all of us," he said. He didn't sound hopeful. He repeated the President's words. "And we'll meet again soon, I think."

The manilla envelope lay on the floor of my study. Its contents were spread on my desk. I had leafed through the lot, the photographs, the attached explanatory notes, the copies of newspaper clippings, the timetable of Melanie's movements from just before Christmas. Every item was numbered and arranged in logical order; every item helped to support the President's story, as he had said it would. Someone—I assumed it was Paul Brill—had done a magnificent job. I was appalled. I got up and poured myself a whisky and soda. Then slowly and painstakingly I went through everything again.

There were two clippings from the *Washington Post*. One was a report of a speech which Melanie had made, blaming the Western Allies for not giving moral and material support to the States in its continued fight to stop the spread of communism; the last paragraph stated that Senator and Mrs. Noel Seabourne had later given a reception in honour of Dr. Lowrey in the picture gallery of their beautiful Georgetown home. The other was from a well-known gossip column and read: "That gay bachelor from the State Department, Mr. John Coller, is in town again. He was a guest at a reception given by Senator 'Nuke-them-all' and Alicia Seabourne to honour Dr. Melanie Lowrey. She is the sister of the British Ambassador to Canada, where John is presently *en poste*." The accompanying photograph showed Melanie and Coller toasting each other; on the wall behind them was what looked to me like a Matisse.

A couple more photographs—Coller showing Melanie the sights of Washington—were superfluous, especially as the quality of the prints was poor. The point had already been established. My sister had known John Coller before she came to Ottawa, before the incident in *The Canada Goose*, before Walter Eland had "introduced" them. I still found it very difficult to believe.

Angrily I turned my attention to Ottawa and the little yellow car.

The Austin American had been hired in the usual way from its usual car-hire firm by the U.S. Embassy, for the personal use of Dr. Melanie Lowrey. The firm had volunteered that the Embassy often hired cars for visiting firemen. The car had been delivered, as asked for, to the home of Mrs. Alex Stocker on the Tuesday before Christmas; the reason given for the Stockers' address was that there was no room in the garage of the British Residence. (That was the first definite untruth I had come across). There were two pictures of the car with its canary-coloured body and blue and white Ontario licence plates. In one Coller and Melanie were taking skis down from the ski-rack; in the other he was holding the door while she got into the driver's seat. Paul had attached a note to say that all information about the car had been checked and was accurate. I didn't doubt it.

How could I? With a jaundiced eye I looked at the remaining photographs. If I had wanted further confirmation of the President's story, here it was. Three of the photographs showed the classic seduction scene, a rug in front of a roaring fire—the inside of Coller's ski-hut, according to the captain—and Melanie and John Coller making love to each other. In the fourth photograph the setting was the same but the woman under Coller was Sally Stocker.

I couldn't think why the President hadn't called me a liar to my face.

CHAPTER 2

January 2

"SO YOU'VE FOUND out about me and John," Melanie said. "I knew you would, of course, sooner or later. I must admit, I hoped it would be later. Then I might have avoided the dénouement," she laughed.

I could have smacked her face.

I wasn't feeling my best after only three hours' sleep, and that sprawled over my desk. Gaby had found me a short while ago, dead to the world. She had had to shake me awake. A shower, a quick shave and a change of clothes had helped—but not much. Meanwhile Gaby had awoken Melanie and made us some tea. It was now six A.M.

"I suppose it was the Canary."

"What?"

"My little yellow car that I've been keeping at the Stockers'. Did Alex give me away in a fit of conscience? It wouldn't have been Sally."

"No."

"Then who was it? You did know about the car?"

"Yes." I tossed the two relevant photographs across the desk. "My informant was the President of Canada. And, as you can see, he produced evidence."

"The President! Oh Mark, you must be—No, you're not joking, are you?" Her voice had changed. She looked quickly from me to Gaby and back again. "My dears, I'm sorry. This is serious for you, is it?"

"It's serious for all of us. I'm not sure yet how serious."
My temper snapped. "Melanie, how could you have been
so bloody stupid?"

"But what have I done? Is it a crime to have a lover in
this city?" She was amused again.

"And is that all you've done, taken a lover?"

"Mark!" Gaby said, in warning or protest. "Melanie, how
long have you known John Coller?"

"Not long, I know." Melanie shrugged. "But I was attracted to him the first time I saw him. That lovely astrakhan
hat! Then Walter introduced us the same evening; ironical
it should have been old Walter." She hesitated. "There's
something I should tell you, perhaps. I should have told
you before, but—pride, I suppose. It's about Colin." Colin
was her Oxford professor. "We were meant to be going to
Malta for Christmas, as you know, but he called it off. Then
he wrote to me in Washington. He hadn't the guts to tell
me to my face, not even after all the years we'd been
together. He's married one of his pupils, a little tart twenty
years younger than he is. He *married* her. And I—" Her
mouth twisted. "Damn him!"

Suddenly, unexpectedly, Melanie began to cry. Gaby went
to her and put her arms around her. She cried like a child
in great noisy sobs, her face screwed up. I hadn't seen her
cry like that since she was twelve and our mother died.
Poor Melanie. All my anger against her evaporated.

I sat and stared at the incriminating photographs, waiting
for her to get control of herself. She would have to tell me
the truth, the whole truth, and perhaps something could be
salvaged. The President hadn't been unsympathetic. He might
be persuaded that she had been no worse than a fool. A lot
would depend on how much of a fool she had been.

"I'm sorry," she said at last. "I didn't mean to make such
a bloody idiot of myself." She wiped her eyes and blew her
nose; her *crise de nerfs* was over. "Mark, I still don't see
what my love-life has to do with the President. What did
he say exactly?"

I told her almost word for word what I had told Gaby
earlier, and she listened attentively. She didn't try to interrupt. When I had finished speaking she said quietly: "Now

I understand why you were so angry with me. The communists have been using me to frame you and John. And I've played right into their hands. But if I've done you dirt, Mark, it hasn't been intentional. Please believe that. And what's more I've not been such a purblind idiot as I'm being made to appear. They've had to improvise a lot." She began to run a hand through her hair and suddenly stopped as she realized she was wearing curlers under a chiffon scarf. "God—God damn them!" she said. She sounded as if she was going to cry again. "Mark, can we have a drink?"

"Of course, what would you like?"

"Champagne," Gaby said firmly. "It's the only possible thing at six o'clock in the morning. I'll get it."

By the time she returned with the champagne I had got Melanie's story straight. It was very simple. She had never seen or heard of John Coller before she came to Ottawa. They had met at Walter's party and then snowmobiling with the Kings. They had been mutually attracted. The attraction had blossomed overnight into an affair. That was natural enough; Melanie was on the rebound and Coller, I suspected, was a womanizer. She would have made no secret of it, Melanie assured me, if I hadn't insisted Coller was an untouchable merely because he was in CIA. The same applied to the car. I had refused to let her rent one in case she had an accident and, as a car was essential for her meetings with Coller, she had had to appeal to Sally Stocker. According to Melanie, Sally knew nothing about her and Coller. Sally had been ready to help because, so she said, I was being a fuss-pot and a spoilsport; it sounded typical of Mrs. S. to me. As for Washington, Melanie hadn't been near the Agency or the State Department and she had not gone sight-seeing with John Coller. The pictures were a fake, which was perhaps why the faces were blurred.

"What about this one?" I said, passing her the photograph reportedly taken at the residence of Senator "Nuke-them-all" Seabourne. "You were at the Seabournes' party?"

"Yes. Yes, I was. It was meant to be in my honour. But John wasn't. And yet—it doesn't make sense. This *is* me and John and this *is* the Seabournes' gallery. I recognize that painting. It's a Matisse, their latest acquisition. Everyone was talking about it. Mark, I don't know how it was done but I swear—"

"What is it?"

"I can prove it's a fake, if I've still got the bill. I never wore that dress at the Seabournes' or anywhere in Washington. I couldn't have done. I bought it at Lord & Taylor's in New York, on my way to Ottawa. And the first time I wore it was at Walter's party." She was triumphant.

"Well, that's a piece of welcome news," I said. "Our enemy has made one mistake, at any rate."

But it seemed to be the only one and it wasn't nearly enough. There was still the notice in the gossip column, the other photographs, and all that Melanie had admitted. I couldn't expect the President to accept her word that nothing more was at stake than a casual love-affair, or my word that, from the moment it was known my sister was spending Christmas with us, she had been used to provide circumstantial evidence that I, the British Ambassador in Ottawa, was having some sort of dealings with American Intelligence. I needed proof of such conspiracy and somehow I had to get it. Before anything else, however, reluctant though I was, I would have to telephone Woods-Dawson.

Woods-Dawson's response, as I had expected, was blistering but at least he didn't spend much time over it. In a disaster Nanny's function was to pick me up, dust me down and set me on my feet again; and Nanny didn't fail me now. By eight o'clock, with the problem dissected and a plan made, I was ready for action. I had even had breakfast.

First I telephoned Alex Stocker. He answered himself, his mouth full of cereal. I could almost hear it going snap, crackle, pop as he hurried to swallow it.

"Two things, Alex," I said cheerfully. "One, my chauffeur will be coming around to your house this morning to collect the Austin America you've been garaging for my sister so kindly. Please make sure he has no difficulty getting it."

"Of course. Yes. Hang on, will you?" There was a long

pause, which made me impatient. Then Alex returned. "Sally will be in until twelve."

"Good. The other thing is—"

"I'm sorry about this business with the car, Mark. I should have told you but the women persuaded me not to. You know how it is. You do understand?"

"I understand. The other thing is that I may not be in today. I don't know how busy you are, but..." I gave him various instructions and rang off before he could begin asking questions. It wouldn't hurt him to stew a little.

Besides, I didn't have time to waste. This was Ottawa, not Whitehall. The government starts work early here—even senior civil servants are at their desks by nine—and I wanted to catch Walter Eland before he left for the office. His telephone rang and rang.

My thoughts wandered to John Coller. He was a separate problem, he and Melanie—and the Stockers. I hadn't told Melanie about Sally yet but I should have to. At least it would bring her relations with Coller to natural end; she wouldn't like the idea of being ridden tandem. And what would Coller's reactions be? I didn't understand Coller. He wasn't green like Melanie. He must have known there was a risk in his relationship with her. Hadn't he cared or, as Woods-Dawson seemed to think, was CIA playing some deep game of its own?

"Yes?"

It was a short, brisk bark which brought me back to the present with a sense of relief. "Walter—I'm so glad I've caught you."

"I'm sorry. I was having a shower. I'm almost on my way to Uplands."

"Uplands? You're not leaving town?" Relief had turned to dismay.

"I'm catching the shuttle to Toronto. I've got meetings this morning at the Canadian Institute and this afternoon with Professor Fraser at the U. of T. Then the weekend with friends. I'll be back on Monday."

"Monday won't do. I must see you—now."

"Mark, I can't manage it. I would if—"

"Please! It's desperately important."

"Okay. Could you drive me to the airport? We could talk on the way."

"Of course. I'll be with you in fifteen minutes. And thanks, Walter."

I put down the receiver. I would have half an hour to convince Walter to abandon his trip and postpone his meetings. The prospects were not good.

I said that Woods-Dawson and I had dissected the problem; we had done more than that. We had devised a whole new scenario which explained nearly all the odd incidents that had happened since Melanie's arrival in Ottawa. Starting from the assumption that the enemy's object was to ensnare my sister and John Coller, we hadn't found it so difficult.

I had first heard of John Coller at that press conference when I had failed to deny that he was Melanie's "close friend from Washington." The question, of course, had been planted so that the names of Dr. Melanie Lowrey and Mr. John Coller would be linked in people's minds. The same was true of the false caption under the photograph of Alice and the White Rabbit at the National Arts Centre Ball; few would bother to read the newspaper's correction, as Walter himself had lamented. Moreover, the confusion had helped to interest Melanie and John Coller in each other even before they met.

Then there had been that business in *The Canada Goose*. It was clear now why nothing had been planted on the woman who had looked enough like Melanie in her fur coat and red-coloured hat to be mistaken for her. It hadn't been necessary or desirable. All that had been needed was for Melanie to be accused and for Coller to come to her rescue; that would have made an excellent basis for a quick friendship and Coller, being Coller, could be expected to go to the help of an attractive woman—indeed, it seemed of any woman. As it was, Melanie had been somewhat taken by "Astrakhan Hat."

And they were to meet the same evening at Walter Eland's party, the next day snowmobiling with the Kings and the day after that ski-ing with the Stockers. Melanie had told him she would be skiing at Camp Fortune and he had followed her. By then they were both hooked. The rest was predictable. The communists had nothing to do but sit and wait—and laugh.

But they hadn't achieved all this by luck alone. It had taken precise, careful planning and they had had help. The help had come, perhaps unwillingly, from someone close to me, someone who would know what the Lowreys would be doing and when and where. I remembered the anonymous telephone caller who had warned me to trust nobody, neither old friends nor new friends. Coller was obviously the new friend, and the old friend—? I was guessing but I would have been happy to believe that by telephoning a warning he was trying to repair some of the damage which he himself had done.

"Sir Mark!"

"What is it?" I awoke with a start. The chauffeur was bending over me, his face anxious.

"Are you all right, sir?"

"Yes. I was just dozing. I had a very short night."

He smiled sympathetically. "Shall I go in and collect Mr. Eland?"

"Please."

I had hoped for a couple of minutes to wipe the sleep away but he reappeared almost at once, carrying Walter's weekend bag. Walter must have been waiting in the foyer. He got into the car beside me and wished me good-morning. It already felt like midday to me.

"Do you wish to go by the Driveway, Sir Mark?"

"Yes."

I wasn't interested in the scenic route, but it was longer and I was going to need all the time I could get.

Walter settled back in his seat and looked at me. "Well, Mark," he said, "why did you need to see me so urgently?"

I returned his gaze and half smiled. I found it difficult to begin. But the Rolls was already moving. The moment had come. I settled for shock tactics.

I said: "Walter, how much do you love Melanie?"

He was obviously surprised at my breach of manners; I had made an unwarranted intrusion on his privacy and Walter was a very private person. Nevertheless, he treated my question with respect. He answered it simply and fully, assuming that his answer was of the utmost importance or I would never have asked it.

"I love her very much, more than I've ever loved any other woman. I'd marry her if she'd have me. However, she turned me down in London—twice. I've considered asking her again before she goes back to Oxford but so far I haven't had the courage. She hasn't given me any reason to believe she has changed her mind, and I'm afraid a third refusal might be horribly final."

"And what's your opinion of John Coller?"

"John Coller?" There was a pause, a long pause. "I scarcely know the man." He was puzzled by the juxtaposition of my questions.

"We met him at your party."

Walter gave a wry laugh. "So did I. And the second time I met him—the only other time—was at your Christmas Eve reception."

"But if you didn't know him what made you invite him?"

"I didn't—not formally. He turned up with a letter that had been put into his mail-box by mistake. He lives in my apartment block, you know; a lot of diplomats do. And it seemed churlish not to ask him in for a drink."

"How odd! He just happened to bring you this letter in the middle of your party?" I sounded disbelieving.

"Not particularly odd." Walter frowned. "Mail does get into wrong boxes sometimes. And it was as easy for Coller to deliver it himself as to give it to the Superintendent the next morning—the office shuts at five—especially as he'd started to open it and wanted to apologize. I've done the same thing myself."

"Was it an important letter?"

"It was an invitation to a reception at the Polish Embassy. I didn't go, if you're interested."

That made sense, excellent sense. It hadn't been a foolproof way of getting Coller to Walter's party but it was comparatively simple. Whoever had arranged it probably knew Coller's movements as well as he knew Melanie's.

And anyway the gambit had worked. Walter had introduced Melanie to John Coller, alias "Astrakhan Hat," her old and close friend from Washington. Once again I was appalled at the thoroughness which had gone into all this planning.

"Mark, we've driven more than half way to Uplands in this beautiful Rolls your government provides for you while you've asked and I've answered extraordinary questions. Now would you please tell me what it's all about?"

I told him. I left out quite a lot. I didn't mention Woods-Dawson or that John Coller was in the Central Intelligence Agency. And, to spare his feelings, I blurred Melanie's precise relationship with Coller, though he must have guessed. He listened in grim silence, pulling at his moustache.

"God damn them," he said when I stopped talking. "God damn the bastards' souls." He swore for a full half minute. Walter never swore.

"I need your help," I said.

"My help—what for?" He didn't wait for an answer. "Mark, there's something I must tell you, in the strictest confidence. It could be worth my job. But the position's worse than you know. Coller—Coller's in CIA. The State Department's only his cover."

"I know," I said gently, appreciating why he had hesitated so long when I asked his opinion of Coller. "Your President told me."

"The President told you that too." He shook his head. "I'm sorry, Mark, but I find the whole thing difficult to take, not intellectually but emotionally. And that Melanie should be so—so involved."

"There's more."

"What?"

I told him about the anonymous telephone calls that I had had and my other reasons for believing that someone close to us had been providing information. He agreed with my conclusions until I narrowed my suspicions to one person. That he wouldn't accept.

"Why him, for heaven's same?" Walter demanded.

"There's a certain amount of circumstantial evidence and

I have to start somewhere."

"Why not with me? How do you know I wasn't black-mailed into it? They always say bachelors are a poor security risk."

"I didn't discount you, Walter. Gaby did. She said it was ridiculous to consider that you would ever do anything to hurt Melanie. It seemed to me a valid point. And I've just checked it with you."

"Bless her," he said. "She's right too. I'd never hurt Melanie."

"But would you do something to help her, to prove she's innocent of any plotting with the Americans?" I was urgent. From the car window I looked across a wide expanse of snow to the airport building; in five minutes we would be at Uplands. "Listen, Walter, this is a ploy on the part of the communists to damage relations between Canada and Britain even more than . . ."

He was still listening when the Rolls drew up at the kerb. His face was expressionless. I had no idea what he was thinking—and little hope. It wasn't until I had put into words what I wanted him to do that I realized how prepos-terous it was. Edgar King was Walter's oldest friend; he had known him most of his life. They were even distantly re-lated. Moreover, Edgar was a trusted colleague in External Affairs, a fellow Canadian. And I, the British Ambassador, was asking Walter to trick Edgar into a confession of what amounted to treason. I was out of my mind.

The chauffeur was standing on the pavement, waiting to open the door. Walter picked up his briefcase. His back was half turned to me and he didn't look around. He spoke over his shoulder.

"I'll be as quick as I can but the sooner I call my secretary the sooner she can cancel my Toronto appointments. And I'll get her to arrange a meeting with Edgar later in the day at my apartment."

He was out of the car and striding towards the glass doors of the air terminal before I could speak. I sat back in my corner, more than happy to wait for him. God knows what had ultimately tipped the balance in my favour. It didn't

really matter. Walter was going to help, and if in the circumstances anyone could extract the truth from Edgar, it
would be Walter. I could scarcely believe my good fortune.

CHAPTER 3

January 2, evening

FROM THE WINDOW of Walter's living-room we looked over the snow-burdened city to the dark distance of the Gatineau hills. To our right, on the far side of the frozen canal, floodlit for the skaters, were the castellated residences of Ottawa University, their roofs decorated with Christmas trees; to our left were towering blocks of apartments and government offices. And immediately in front, beyond the buildings and the playing field of Lisgar Collegiate where some students were making a giant snowman, we could see National Defence headquarters, the oxidized copper towers of the Château Laurier and the mass of the Parliament Buildings. We could even tell the time from the bright face of the Peace Tower clock. It was twenty-two minutes past five, the rush hour, and the driveways were a moving ribbon of car lights.

This was a scene that Walter knew and loved, but it obviously wasn't much comfort to him tonight. His gaze was unseeing and his fingers tapped on the window-pane, on and on. The nervous little rhythm had me worried. If I was wrong about Edgar I would have wasted a whole day; but if I was right and Walter failed to make him confess to it I would have come to a dead end. I passed a hand over my face, which felt vaguely bruised from lack of sleep.

The telephone shrilled and we both jumped. We were a fine pair of conspirators. I could imagine Woods-Dawson's scorn if he could have seen us.

"No, that's okay," Walter said. "Six o'clock, then." He put down the receiver. "He's been held up but he hopes to be here by six. He says he can't stay long. They're going out to dinner and Heather'll kill him if he's late home."

"He's coming. That's all that matters," I said. "I was afraid he was going to cry off."

"No, he wouldn't do that. I asked him to come as a— a personal favour." Walter winced. "Oh God, how I hope you're wrong. I'll gladly lick his boots."

"I'm not wrong," I said, with far more assurance than I felt. "And this is the only way. He'd never confide in anybody but you." I managed an encouraging grin. "Do you think it's too soon to make me comfortable? We don't want a sudden panic if he arrives early."

"And he might do just that. You're right. I'll go and get your chair and we'll fix you up."

I went and inspected the kitchen, which was a long narrow space taken out of the L-shaped living-room. One of its doors led into the hall and the other into the dining area. Both of them were louvred, which meant that at least I wouldn't have to sit in darkness, but they didn't enable me to see more than a foot of carpet beyond them and I wouldn't be able to watch Edgar. However, there was nowhere else to hide.

Walter brought a small, rather hard armchair from the bedroom. It fitted with inches to spare between the dishwasher and the refrigerator. I sat down and wriggled in my seat. The next hour or so promised to be mentally and physically uncomfortable. But it would be worth it if only . . .

"Will you be all right?" Walter asked anxiously.

"Yes. Don't worry about me," I said. "Concentrate on Edgar. And whatever you do, don't forget to turn on the tape-recorder."

"I won't. I'm going to shut you up now so I can check that there's no sign of you through the kitchen doors. Okay?"

"Right. Walter."

"Yes?"

"Good luck." It was the wrong thing to say but I couldn't think what else.

"Thanks." His voice was dry.

Alone in the semi-darkness I tried to make my body relax.
I could hear Walter moving around the living-room and the
hall. By turning my head I could see the large round face
of the electric clock whose hands seemed to advance in
alarming jerks. At five minutes to six the buzzer sounded
forcefully. Edgar had arrived.

There was a pause—and a sharp click as Walter turned
on the tape-recorder. Then came the opening and shutting
of the front-door, the casual greetings and the inevitable
winter delay while Edgar took off his overboots and his
heavy outer clothes. At last they were walking to the far
end of the living-room and Walter was suggesting that they
sat down.

"Pity you had to cancel your Toronto trip," Edgar said.
"I hope you're not in for a bout of flu?" Walter had invented
a sudden indisposition to explain his movements. "You certainly look a bit off-colour. How are you feeling?"

"Not too bad," Walter said.

"Then what about a drink? I don't know about you but
I could do with a Scotch. It's been a lousy day."

I half listened to the movements in the living-room and
the tiny sounds that are part of making a whisky and soda.
Ice! Suddenly I found myself gripping the arms of my chair.
Edgar would expect ice. But I was sitting beside the refrigerator. If Walter came into the kitchen by the door of
the dining-L Edgar would see me and if Walter went around
by the hall, an absurd thing to do, Edgar would want to
know why. He would follow and find me. Slowly I got to
my feet. It was better to confront Edgar than to be exposed.

My hand was outstretched to push open the door when
Walter spoke. His voice was as clear as if he had been
standing beside me. "Here you are Edgar," he said. "I've
made it a double. What I want to talk about is so unpleasant
that we need some Dutch courage."

I drew a deep breath and allowed it gently to escape,
unable to believe I could have been so stupid as to forget
that Walter had filled the ice bucket. Then very cautiously
I sat down again and wiped the palms of my sweating hands
on my trouser legs. I was ashamed of having panicked. I
set myself to concentrate on what was being said.

"Edgar, you and I have been friends for a long time, haven't we?"

"For over thirty years. God, how old we are!"

"And you know that if ever you were in any difficulty I'd rally around, do what I could to help?"

"Yes, of course, but——"

"So why didn't you come to see me? I would've helped. You know I would. We could've worked something out together. At least we could've tried."

"I don't know what you're talking about, Walter."

"You're deep in trouble, Edgar, aren't you?"

"No. What makes you think I am?"

"If a foreign service officer starts knocking back whisky as you've been doing lately, it's a sure sign that something's wrong. And don't tell me it's Christmas."

"As far as I'm concerned, what's wrong is that I'm overworked at the office and nagged at home. Heather's always wanting something for the kids or the house or herself. And the latest thing, as you know perfectly well, is that I'm overdue for a posting. She practically gave me a choice of three posts which were going to be up for grabs. You've got the best of them. If I don't make ambassador in one of the others, God help me. I won't be able to show my mug around the house any more."

"Heather—yes."

"What do you mean by that?"

"I was just thinking that Heather and her ambitions must have made things doubly hard for you in Prague."

There was a gobbling sound from Edgar. I could picture him with his sandy hair and his freckles and his little boy face which would be suffused with an ugly redness. He would be sitting bolt upright with his chin tucked into his neck and his eyes blinking. But these could merely be signs of suppressed emotions; I had seen him like that on occasions when Heather had goaded him too far. They weren't necessarily signs of guilt.

"Well, that's where it began, wasn't it, Edgar? In Prague," Walter said gently. "That's when you started working for the communists. They set you up and compromised you. You should have asked to be brought home at once—you know the form—but you didn't, because you couldn't face Heather. And the Reds didn't want much of you. They never do in the beginning. Wasn't that how it happened, Edgar?"

The silence grew heavy and I found myself biting my lower lip. This was the critical point. Prague was a guess. But Prague had been Edgar's last post, the only one he had had behind the Iron Curtain, and the dates fitted. It was a reasoned guess. And it was right. Edgar didn't even try to deny it.

"Yes," he said dully. "That's how it happened. How—how did you know?" His voice was strangled. "I want another Scotch."

I stopped gritting my teeth. Tension flowed out of me. I had been right. Thank God, I had been right! Edgar was guilty and he had admitted it. Now, by proving conspiracy, he would clear both Melanie and myself, the President would be satisfied that there had been no Anglo-American collusion and I would have escaped the communist trap. I felt weak with gratitude.

Walter was getting Edgar his whisky. He was moving about the room because when he next spoke I didn't catch what he said. I strained to listen. Edgar had mumbled some reply; he sounded as if his head was buried in his hands. For a full minute I suffered my frustration. Then Walter's voice came loud and clear—and full of pity.

". . . you must tell me about it or I can't help."

"You can't help anyway. Nobody can."

"Of course I can. And I will. I promise." It was impossible to doubt Walter's sincerity. "But you must co-operate. First tell me what the communists have got on you."

"All right."

It wasn't an original story. Edgar had gone to an official reception without Heather and, in the course of the evening, had felt unwell; in retrospect he thought that someone might have drugged his drink. He had gone to the lavatory and passed out. Several hours later he had woken up in a strange room. He was lying on a bed beside a very handsome boy aged about fourteen. They were both naked and it was apparent that they had made love. Edgar had been horrified. He had leapt from the bed, found his clothes neatly folded on a chair in an outer room, dressed as quickly as he could and fled.

For two weeks he had lived in terror but nothing had happened. Then he had received, through the post, a package containing photographs, with the gratuitous information that copies would be sent to his wife and his ambassador unless he did as he was told; he was to give a dinner party to which he was to ask certain people. It seemed a small price to pay.

"Of course there were other—requests," Edgar said bitterly. "But none of them was awful. I made some introductions and I provided some information. Nothing of any value. Statistics mainly that they could have got out of the Canada Year Book. Then I was posted home. I—I tried to kid myself that that was an end to it."

"But it wasn't, was it?"

There was silence. He didn't answer.

"Edgar, it wasn't the last thing they asked of you, was it?" Walter persisted.

"It was—right up until April of this year, after our holiday in Jamaica. That was when everything went wrong. My brother was nearly killed, you remember, and Ma was ill and they—they started on me again."

"When they heard that Mark Lowrey was to be the first British Ambassador to Canada."

"You know?"

"Not in detail. Tell me."

So Edgar told him and, unknowingly, me and the tape-recorder. Everything spewed out of him.

It was worse than I had imagined. Every single fact about me and my family that he knew or could dredge up from his memory he had passed on to my enemy. Some were stupid things such as that Gaby refused to wear fur and that once, at the tender age of six, I had jumped into the Round Pond in Kensington Gardens to rescue Melanie who had fallen in. Some were vaguely more sinister such as details of Colette's life in Jersey, including the approximate date on which she hoped to make me a grandfather. But Edgar had been ordered to prepare a report in depth and nothing was to be left out. The thought revolted me.

And once Gaby and I were in Ottawa there had been orders to get as close to us as possible. We hadn't made it difficult. The communists must have known almost as soon as I did that Melanie would be spending Christmas with us. They had been able to make their plans accordingly.

Inevitably, more had been demanded of Edgar. Not only did he have to continue to spy on us, but he had to steal a selection of our invitation cards and writing paper, provide copies of our handwriting, and later arrange a snowmobiling party to include "all the Lowreys and that bastard John Coller." (Clearly Edgar had had nothing to do with setting up the American; on the contrary he seemed to think that Coller had co-operated voluntarily with the communists, which accounted for his dislike of the man.) He had also been told to take photographs of Coller at our Christmas Eve party, preferably talking to myself or Gaby. But this last he had failed to do.

There was a pause and Edgar said miserably. "You must think me an awful shit, Walter, but it was the Lowreys or the Kings and—Oh, what the hell! I did what I could for Mark. I called him—twice. Once to warn him to be on his guard and the second time to tell him all the funny business was over, the communists had got what they wanted."

"That must have been a consolation for him," Walter said drily, but my heart warmed to Edgar; I had half suspected he might be my anonymous caller.

"For Chrissakes, Walter! Do you have to rub my nose in it?"

"I'm sorry."

"I got Paul Brill to come to that snowmobiling party too. Paul didn't stop Mark getting shot at, I know, but he did get the police off our backs. And I hoped perhaps, if he and Mark got together . . ."

In the semi-darkness of the kitchen I shifted in my chair. Carefully I uncrossed my legs, trying to make myself a little less uncomfortable, and without warning a sharp pain ran up my calf, knotting the muscles. The cramp was excruciating. I gritted my teeth and began to massage my leg. The pain refused to ease. Gingerly I stood up. I yearned to stamp my foot, to stride into the living-room and march its length. Instead I endured but the wretched pain was so intense that it absorbed me. It was minutes before I could concentrate again.

Walter was saying: ". . . a scandal like that's the last thing the President'll want. Once he's convinced that the Brits and the Yanks have only been made to appear to be scheming together he'll be eager to keep the whole affair under wraps. You'll have to resign from External, of course, and Heather won't like that but, good God, Edgar, in the circumstances it's a small price, isn't it?"

"I suppose so," Edgar said flatly. "But they'll still have the Prague photographs."

"Worthless once you're out of the government service, surely."

"And what about John Coller?"

"What about him? He doesn't know you're involved."

"I bet he does. The bloody communist! I barely knew him and yet when I invited him out of the blue to go snow-mobiling he accepted at once. He didn't even pretend to be surprised at the invitation."

Walter laughed wearily. "Honestly, Edgar, I'm sure we don't have to worry about Coller."

"Why not?" Edgar persisted. "If the man's a communist something should be done about him."

"Edgar, Coller's—" Walter stopped. It was clear to me, listening, that he didn't want to be responsible for telling Edgar that Coller was in fact in CIA. "Forget Coller. I'll cope with that problem. Let's get down to writing this statement of yours. Come along, I'll dictate if you—"

"I want another drink first. And make it a good strong one. Then I'll write and sign any damn thing you like. Why not? To hell with everything. I'm beyond caring what happens."

I gave up listening and began to massage my leg again. I let my thoughts range free. Gradually I relaxed. And, incredible as it may seem, while Walter and Edgar sweated over a written statement of Edgar's guilt, I slept.

I didn't wake until Walter came into the kitchen to say that Edgar had gone.

CHAPTER 4

January 3

THE NEXT MORNING, if I didn't feel like a new man, I felt decidedly better than I had twenty-four hours ago. Nothing was a quarter as grim as it had been then. And, in spite of a warning from Woods-Dawson that the pattern of events was unlikely to be as simple as it now appeared, I was in an optimistic mood when I went down to breakfast. I should have had more sense.

The telephone rang while I was still at the toast and marmalade stage. Alex Stocker needed to see me as soon as possible. Something had come up, he said, something vital that he wasn't prepared to discuss on an open line. When I asked for a hint he said it was concerned with a friend of Melanie's. That set me back. He had to mean John Coller and I couldn't afford to ignore any gossip that Alex might have got hold of if it was about Melanie and Coller. I told him I would see him in my office at ten o'clock.

Yesterday had been such a waste as regards Her Majesty's chores that I had planned to go into the Chancery this morning even though it was Saturday; I wanted to catch up with the telegrams and whatever else there might be before meeting Paul Brill at Walter's apartment. And when Alex arrived, I was beavering away at my desk. He had interrupted my prose at a crucial moment but I did my best not to seem unwelcoming. He sat down opposite me, heavy with mystery, and I wondered what was coming. Nothing. I didn't have time to spend on pregnant silences.

I said abruptly: "You want to tell me something about John Coller?"

"Ah, then you knew I meant Coller when I referred to Melanie's friend." He sounded triumphant.

All I could do was ignore my own stupidity. "Well," I said, "what about him?"

But Alex wasn't to be hurried. "Mark, I appreciate that it's none of my business whom anyone in your family chooses to be friends with and in the normal course of events I wouldn't dream of mentioning it. Indeed I haven't mentioned it, except of course to Sally." He was in full spate now and I didn't interrupt. "All my sympathies were with your sister over her little yellow car. It seemed to me absurd, if you don't mind my saying so, that you wouldn't allow her to hire a car in Ottawa if she wanted to. And once I'd seen her with John Coller it was obvious why she did want to."

"I don't understand."

"It was just chance I happened to see him get out of her car."

"Presumably she'd given him a lift."

"He put his head in the window and kissed her goodbye — on the lips."

I swallowed that one. Alex knew that Melanie and Coller were quote friends unquote and he had told Sally; he told Sally everything. This was unfortunate but I couldn't see why it should be important. Nevertheless, I had a nasty feeling that it might be.

"As I said, I wouldn't have mentioned it, only it appears that Mr. John Coller is in actual fact a member of the Central Intelligence Agency."

"Good God!" He had exploded his bombshell and I had to feign surprise.

Alex smiled. "That puts a different complexion on things, doesn't it?"

"Who told you?"

"We were at a dinner party last night and everyone seemed to know. Ottawa's buzzing with the news."

Now he had surprised me. "It mightn't be true," I said weakly.

"It probably is. And anyhow does that matter? The US Goverment's bound to deny it—at least to begin with. But they'll withdraw him in the end, you'll see. They won't have any choice. There's going to be a frightful stink over this, Mark. The Yanks are unpopular enough already and you know how touchy the Canadians are about any threat to their beloved sovereignty. They won't take kindly to CIA operating north of the border. They never have."

"One can scarcely blame them," I said absently, my mind on the implications of Coller's blown cover.

"And it won't do us any good to be mixed up in this business. The Canucks don't exactly love us either at the moment. Any excuse—"

"Why on earth should we be mixed up in it?"

"Well, if it became known that John Coller and Melanie—" Not quite meeting my eye, he gave me what was meant to pass as a sympathetic grin. "Melanie is your sister, Mark, and you are the British Ambassador. It does make you vulnerable."

It most certainly did. I knew that, better than he did. But I didn't like being threatened, least of all by my own Minister. With considerable self-restraint I told myself that Alex was just making a point—if my sister was playing around with a member of CIA in Ottawa I was no pot to call him kettle-black because of his wife's comparatively minor misdeeds. Alex, in fact, was merely getting his own back on Sally's behalf. If only he had known about her and Coller ... I felt a surge of exasperated pity for him—and a momentary yearning to clout him.

Restraining both emotions, however, I got rid of him as quickly as possible, cleared up my papers and left the Chancery for my appointment with Walter and Paul Brill.

"Could Stocker be dangerous, do you think?" Walter asked. We were drinking instant coffee in his apartment and waiting for Paul, who was late.

"No, not really," I said. "After all, one doesn't get to

the rank of Minister in the British Foreign Service without some sense of responsibility."

"I don't like it. I don't like Stocker knowing about Melanie and Coller."

"He doesn't know much. I pointed out that a farewell kiss is a pretty trivial matter."

"Not if there's going to be a major row over Coller and the communists want to involve her." Walter was insistent.

I heaved a sigh. "I'd be happier if I were sure that Coller getting blown at this particular moment was just chance," I said. I could hear the echo of Woods-Dawson in my voice and wished that I had his prescience. As usual, he had been right: the solution wasn't going to be as simple as it had seemed . . .

Walter broke in on my brooding. "Mark, I have a suggestion to make. Actually it occurred to me in the—er—night and I've given it considerable thought." He was pink in the face with embarrassment. "It seems a better idea than ever now. I think Melanie and I should become engaged."

"What?" I wrenched my thoughts from the problematic future.

"You heard," he said with gentle dignity. "If our engagement was publicly announced and you gave a—a surprise party for us there would be a lot of local publicity, more than enough to gainsay any rumours about her and Coller. And, naturally, she can break it off as soon as it's convenient. Will you ask her?"

"Yes."

"Explain why it's a good thing. Urge her to agree. I think it could be important."

"Yes," I said again.

The shrilling of the telephone saved my inadequacy from becoming too obvious. But what could I have said? Walter didn't want to be told that my sister was a bloody fool who couldn't recognize a good man when he offered himself. He didn't want thanks or pity. The telephone's interruption couldn't have been more opportune—for both of us.

I stared out of the window. Walter was doing more listening than talking and anyway it wasn't my business. I watched the heavy fat flakes of snow floating relentlessly down from the leaden sky and flattening themselves against the glass, distorting the view which last night had looked so attractive. The weatherman had promised us five to six inches of what he jocularly called "the white stuff." It would be good for the skiers and the snowmobilers. My thoughts turned back to John Coller.

"That was Heather," Walter said, looking worried. "Edgar didn't come home last night. As far as I can make out, nobody's seen him since he left here yesterday. Heather's dreadfully upset. She doesn't know what to do."

"But they were going out to dinner. Edgar said—"

"I know. Heather went ahead. She left him a note but he never joined them."

"What did you tell her?"

"That Edgar was okay when he left me, that he might well have gone back to the East Block, that there was a— a top-secret problem which I couldn't discuss with her. What else could I say?"

"What's she going to do?"

"Well, I told her she should do nothing for the moment. I said I'd make some enquiries and be in touch. I sort of implied it was something to do with his work but I'm not sure she believed me. Mark, what do you think has happened to him?"

"God knows! Most likely he got drunk and is sleeping it off somewhere, maybe in your local pokey. Or I suppose he could've had an accident and been taken to hospital. I don't imagine Heather wants to call the police?"

"Not if it can be avoided, obviously. But I'm worried about him. Aren't you?"

"Yes!"

"And I hate doing nothing."

"Nevertheless, I think we must—do nothing, I mean. Surely it's sensible to give him more time. He's probably waking up in some sleazy hotel across the river or in a brothel somewhere with an appalling hangover and the prospect of explaining to Heather where he's been all night."

"Perhaps. I hope you're right."

This time we were interrupted by the arrival of Paul Brill. He looked yellow-skinned, bleary-eyed, tired and distrait.

He accepted a whisky thankfully. First we discussed John Coller and Paul verified that the story had broken. Later in the day press, radio and television would have an official statement from the US Embassy denying that Coller was or ever had been a member of the Central Intelligence Agency. Nobody would believe it.

"It's the worst possible moment for this to become public," Paul said in sudden exasperation. "If the communists could have picked the time—Forget it!" He gave a lop-sided grin. "You asked me to come here. I gather there's some good news."

"Yes," I said, wondering why this was the worst possible moment. "I can give the President proof that my sister didn't meet Coller until she came to Ottawa. The Washington photographs are faked. For example, the dress she was meant to have worn at Senator Seabourne's party wasn't bought until she got to New York. In Ottawa the communists organized her meeting with Coller and cultivated their relationship. Again there's evidence."

I went into some detail and Paul Brill listened attentively, nodding his head. Occasionally he asked a question. He showed no surprise. I might have been telling him a story of which he already knew the broad outlines.

"I'm hoping," I concluded, "that the President, given proof of my sister having been set up by the communists, will accept her word that her relationship with John Coller was purely social and nothing whatsoever to do with any sort of clandestine communications between the British and the US Governments."

"Yes," he said slowly. "Yes. I think I can assure you of that." He didn't sound particularly happy about it.

He was even less happy when I told him that it was Edgar who had been helping the enemy. By mutual consent neither Walter nor I mentioned that Edgar had disappeared.

"What a mess," he said. "What a goddam mess!"

We didn't contradict him. Later, after he had gone and we were again debating what to do about Edgar, Walter said he had never before seen Paul looking so distraught. He also said that he felt that our meeting with him had been somehow unsatisfactory. As far as I was concerned the whole morning had been unsatisfactory. By now I was once more enveloped in a malaise of uneasiness.

Three hours later I was belting myself into the front seat of the Mercedes that Walter had brought back from his last posting and Walter was edging the car and its trailer out of a warm underground garage into the blizzard outside. As we emerged into the dark of the afternoon he switched on the lights and the windshield wipers, hoping to make some impression on the smothering blanket of snow. They didn't seem to make much difference.

We turned into the Driveway, struck a patch of ice and slid half across the road, missing by inches the huge yellow snow-plough which was already at work. It wasn't an auspicious beginning.

"Sorry!" Walter said.

Behind us my chauffeur settled himself again, more comfortably. He must have been wishing himself at home or, if we had to go into the country on such a day, behind the wheel of the Rolls. But Walter had insisted on taking his own car—the Rolls, he said, was too conspicuous and anyway was not equipped for towing a snowmobile—and I had insisted my chauffeur should come with us. Though I didn't say so to Walter, he was a form of insurance. I wasn't going to walk slap into some new trouble completely unprotected. Not that I was expecting trouble. I don't know what I was expecting. I only knew that I couldn't let Walter go without me even if I weren't the most useful of companions for such an expedition. And, in the event, my chauffeur was to prove invaluable.

"This is a bloody mad undertaking," I said. "You haven't told me yet why Heather's suddenly so sure Edgar has spent the night at his lot."

"She called Edgar's parents in Toronto and his father suggested looking in the closets. It was a bright idea. She found the suit he wore to the office yesterday, but all his snowmobiling gear had gone. He must've been home and changed during the evening."

"I see. Did he take a snowmobile?"

"No. Just his snowshoes—and two bottles of whisky."

"They'll have stopped him from freezing to death overnight."

"Oh, he'll have been warm enough in the hut, unless he got so drunk he burnt it down. But he'll have a ghastly hangover when he wakes and he mayn't be in any fit state to get himself back to Ottawa, especially in this storm. There's always the possibility of an accident, too. He could've twisted an ankle and be lying in the bush somewhere."

It wasn't a pleasant possibility. I thought about it—and the other time that I had gone out to Edgar's lot. What a day that had been! And Edgar must have felt himself responsible. Poor Edgar. He must have been through hell. I hoped we would find him in the hut, safe and warm and almightily hung over.

Walter said: "Did you speak to Melanie about my—er—suggestion?"

"Yes. Yes, I did."

"What did she say?"

I hesitated. I couldn't tell him the truth. In fact, when Melanie had grasped what Walter was really proposing, she had said: "Engaged? To my poor old walrus?" and burst into tears; Gaby and I had had difficulty in persuading her to be practical about it. Fortunately a solitary van, going much too fast for the amount of visibility, chose this moment to overtake us and Walter was distracted from my silence.

"She agreed, I hope?" he said, when the van's tail-lights had disappeared into the grey murk.

"Indeed yes," I said. "She agreed with—with gratitude. She said it was a noble gesture, typical of you." In fact it was Gaby who had said this, not Melanie. I put some more of her words into Melanie's mouth. "She also asked me to invite you to lunch tomorrow."

"Tomorrow? Sunday lunch?" Walter knew my views about keeping Sunday a family day.

"Yes," I said firmly. "It would seem appropriate. And we can discuss details. After all, time is of the essence."

"I'm honoured," he said, with only a tinge of bitterness.

He was driving more and more slowly now, peering through the windshield at what should have been the black highway. In fact the headlights showed only a wide expanse of whiteness. We could have been driving across a snow-covered field into nothingness or, more likely, on to the shoulder of the road and into a deep ditch. There was no other traffic. I hoped Walter knew what he was doing and where he was.

Evidently he did because suddenly, after crawling along for some fifty yards, he swung the Mercedes off the highway and on to the concession road. Here, shut in by the trees, it was already night. Edgar had boasted that his lot was a mere hour's drive from central Ottawa but we had taken almost two to get so far. It was another twenty minutes before we turned on to the dirt track which bordered the Kings' property and Walter drew up at the side.

"I don't think we dare go any further," he said. "But this should be okay. Nobody's likely to run into us and we'll be able to dig ourselves out. I've got sand and a spade in the trunk." Reluctantly we left the comfort of the car and, floundering around in the snow, unloaded the snowmobile and packed it with a combined survival and first-aid kit that included a blanket and a flask of brandy. At the last minute we threw in the spade which was to be absolutely essential. In fact we needed it almost at once.

A hundred yards down the dirt track Edgar's car was parked broadside along the gate which led into his property, the gate on which John Coller had been sitting so happily the last time I had come here. Edgar had taken the keys but fortunately hadn't locked the door. Without a word my chauffeur got into the driving seat, fiddled for a moment, and started the engine. Walter and I pushed. We moved the car. Then the three of us took turns to dig away the snow so that we could open the gate. At least we had the satisfaction of knowing we weren't on a wild goose chase. Edgar had come to the peace of his beloved lot.

Not that it was peaceful today. The wind soughed in the trees and blew damp snow in my face as I huddled on the back seat of the snowmobile, grateful for the protection of Walter's body in front of me and thankful that I wasn't in my chauffeur's place, snowshoeing behind. My skin was still sticky with the sweat of digging but, in spite of it, I felt chilled to the bone. I yearned to get to the hut.

We were taking our problems one by one and hadn't considered what we should do if Edgar wasn't there. He could be anywhere, under any bush, in any snowdrift, dead drunk or just dead from exposure. There wouldn't be any tracks to follow and it would be chance if we found him. Even in summer daylight it would have taken hours to search the lot. Edgar had to be in the hut. Otherwise . . .

When we broke from the trees into the clearing the storm seemed to have abated a little. We roared across the whiteness and drew up by the hut. Walter didn't wait for me. He was out of the snowmobile and hammering on the door. There was no answer. He had tried the handle but the door opened outwards and it was impossible to tell whether it was locked or prevented from opening by the mound of drifted snow which almost reached the keyhole.

Automatically I seized the spade and began to dig. It was heavy, wet, clinging stuff and after a couple of spadesful I was sweating again. I dug and dug until my vision was blurring and my chest hurt; I didn't seem to be making much progress. Someone took the spade from me.

"Let me have a go, sir."

"Thanks."

I leaned against the wall of the hut and tried to control my breathing. My heart thumped erratically. Walter had cleared the snow from the window and was peering through.

"I can't see a thing. If he's inside he must be fast asleep."

"Someone's inside, sir—or has been quite recently. Smoke's still coming from the chimney."

"Smoke? Are you sure?"

"Yes, sir. I saw it in the snowmobile lights as you drove into the clearing."

"Thank God for that!" I said. "He'll be all right then."

"Yes—except for a frightful hangover." Walter laughed with relief.

"The door's free, sir. And it's not locked."

"Splendid."

We crowded into the hut together, glad to be out of the cold and the blowing snow. Inside it was sheltered, several degrees warmer—and darker, until Walter produced a huge flashlight. He switched it on and put it down on the table so that the light shone upwards and the whole inside of the hut was illuminated.

It was much as I had remembered it. There was matting on the floor, chintz curtains, gay cushions, a lot of chairs and a long table on which today were two whisky bottles and a glass. The charred remains of some logs were still smouldering in the grate.

Edgar lay in a strange crumpled heap in front of the fire. The gun was beside his hand. I think he must have pressed the muzzle into the roof of his mouth and pulled the trigger. The result was obscene.

Beside me Walter retched. Then blindly we staggered out of the hut together and vomited into the snow. It was my chauffeur who found the note that Edgar had left, who re-arranged the evidence to make it look like an accident and who stayed in the hut while Walter and I went for the police. Woods-Dawson's man took it all in his stride. He had been more upset when our cat was splattered against the elm, but then he had been fond of Thomas. Edgar had been Walter's friend and mine.

CHAPTER 5

January 4, morning

I DUG AND DUG. The snow seemed to get heavier at every spadeful. And all my effort was useless. The snow melted as soon as it fell upon Edgar's body. I worked harder and faster, doing my best to cover the ghastly mess that had once been his head; but even this wasn't possible. Nevertheless I couldn't stop. I dug and sweated and gasped for breath. Someone was hanging on to my arm which didn't help a bit.

Gaby was shaking me. "Mark, wake up! You must wake up. We're almost at the Cathedral."

"I—I'm sorry."

She must have seen the horror in my eyes. "Oh darling! You were dreaming about Edgar?"

"Yes. Sorry. I didn't sleep too well last night."

She didn't tell me—as Woods-Dawson had done—to stop blaming myself, that Edgar had had something coming to him. She put her arm through mine and squeezed it. "I love you," she said simply. I nodded. I managed to smile at her.

The Rolls drew up in front of the Cathedral and we got out. The pavement had been ploughed and the pathway to the main door of the church shovelled so that we passed between walls of piled snow; the odd flake was still floating down from a leaden sky. We were walking along a red carpet and the thought crossed my mind that it might be in honour of the President, though almost invariably he heard mass in the private chapel of the Palace.

"The Archbishop must be entertaining some illustrious visitors," I said. "I hope we haven't let ourselves in for a party after mass. I don't think I could face it today." I needn't have worried; I wasn't even to see His Grace.

We had scarcely reached the doors of the Cathedral when a monsignor in his long soutane rustled out to greet us. He bowed low and welcomed us to the church. Since we attended mass there every Sunday this seemed to me somewhat overdoing things; maybe it was to compensate for the Archbishop's sudden, brooking-no-refusal invitation that we had received only yesterday. I raised an eyebrow at Gaby behind the priest's back as he led the way down the aisle to one of the front pews.

We had timed it nicely and he had barely glided away when the mass began. I did my best to concentrate but without much success, saying the familiar words automatically while my unhappy thoughts darted all over the place. Occasionally some phrase recalled me, only to set me off on another tangent. During the sermon I didn't even try to listen. Instead I let my mind drift . . .

Gaby's elbow caught me sharply in the ribs. The sacristy bell gave its plaintive call and belatedly I knelt for the oblation of the Host. I prayed. I stood and said the Lord's Prayer with the rest of the congregation. I offered my hand to my neighbour as a sign of peace; he smelt of garlic and I was glad a symbolic kiss wasn't required of me. A little later I received communion, more to please Gaby than from any personal desire. And the mass was over, the final blessing said.

The same priest came to take us to the Archbishop and, I hoped, a pre-prandial drink. As the congregation began to make its way out of the Cathedral he led us through a side door into the vestry and along a corridor painted institutional green. We rounded a corner and there was Paul Brill, the last man I expected to meet at this time and in this place.

"Good morning, Lady Lowrey. Sir Mark," he said stiffly, perhaps for the priest's benefit.

"Morning," I said, omitting his name.

He turned to Gaby. "Lady Lowrey, the Archbishop's expecting you for sherry, I believe. Would you mind going on ahead while I have a few words with His Excellency?"

"No—not at all." Gaby's words belied her obvious reluctance to leave me.

"Is it really necessary—" I was beginning.

"Thank you very much," Paul said and smiled at her. "I hope we shan't be too long."

Feeling out-manoeuvered, I watched Gaby being led away somewhere. Then Paul opened a door and stood aside for me to pass so that I preceded him into a dark, airless room which smelt of furniture polish. Sitting at one end of a long table was the President.

"Sir Mark Lowrey, *Excellence*," Paul announced formally.

Absorbing behind the diplomatic carapace my second surprise in as many minutes, I exchanged greetings with the old man who today, I noticed, was showing his age. For that matter Paul Brill was haggard and unstarched-looking. They didn't need to tell me there was more bad news in store. It was apparent from their weary grimness. What I didn't realize, however, was that the President was about to administer to me the final *coup de grâce*.

"As usual, Sir Mark, there's not much time," he began. "I have to attend the High Mass and I can't be too late because they won't start without me." He grinned sardonically. "Three birds with one stone! I give thanks to my Maker. I demonstrate to my loving public that nobody has yet assassinated me. And—I plot with the British Ambassador."

"I trust that as regards the last of the three birds you are speaking metaphorically, *Excellence*?"

"No, Sir Mark—on the contrary. That's why I arranged for us to meet in this cloak-and-dagger fashion. I considered it essential that our meeting should be held in the highest secrecy. But please convey my apologies to Lady Lowrey for involving her."

Without speaking, I bowed my acquiescence.

"Good. To business, then. First I'm going to recount

what has happened in chronological order and I would ask you, even though you'll be provoked, Sir Mark, not to interrupt me. Some of the story which I have to tell you will fit in with what we were talking about at my skating party on New Year's Day. Please!" He held up his hand as I opened my mouth. "While I'm at mass Paul will show you the material evidence and I'll say right away that we know some of it is false. Afterwards I'll return and we can discuss the extremely serious implications. Now, while I'm talking, perhaps you'll take a glass of sherry."

"Thank you."

I had been aware of Paul moving around in the gloomy room but my attention had been focused on the President and I hadn't noticed the decanter and glasses on a tray until the President mentioned sherry. I would have preferred a long whisky—my mouth was suddenly very dry—but I was grateful for anything. I forced myself to take a sip and put the glass down. I turned to the President and listened.

"Shortly before Christmas," he said, "we received a letter, mailed in Ottawa and composed of words which had been cut out of the local newspapers and pasted on to a sheet of foolscap. It stated that the writer had some information about the Carmine Project which would be of the greatest interest to Canada."

Involuntarily my fingers tightened around the stem of the sherry glass. The Carmine Project! What with Melanie's affaire with John Coller and Edgar's death I had practically forgotten Carmine.

"In the normal course of events," the President continued, "the letter would have been ignored as coming from yet another crank, but with it he sent a photograph, taken in Washington, of John Coller of the Central Intelligence Agency and Dr. Melanie Lowrey soon to visit her brother, the British Ambassador to Canada. This meant that he knew two fascinating pieces of information. He might know more. So we put the ad he had asked for in the miscellaneous column of the evening paper and, having shown interest, we waited.

"The second letter stated that the United Kingdom and the United States were together plotting against Canada. To substantiate this statement he enclosed details of meetings in Ottawa between Coller and yourself and your sister, with more photographs. He said that Dr. Lowrey of her own volition was having an affaire with a United States agent and the British Ambassador was using this affaire for undercover communication with the Americans. He suggested we should check for ourselves. And naturally we did."

The President stopped speaking for a moment to sip his sherry and I seized my chance.

"Excellence, I would like to state categorically that there is no truth whatsoever in the accusation that the UK and the US have been plotting together against Canada," I said firmly. "On the contrary, we are the victims of a communist plot as, I would have thought, Edgar King's statement had made amply clear."

"Please, Sir Mark, please! Let me finish." He looked at his watch and sighed. "All that was really a build-up. He was just setting the stage. Our unknown correspondent has now offered to sell us, for the sum of one hundred thousand dollars, what purports to be an authentic document about the Carmine Project. And he maintains that in view of the vast amount of supporting evidence against you and Mr. Coller—incidentally, he has produced still more—there can be no doubt that it is authentic.

"Sir Mark, this document—we have a Xeroxed copy of only two pages—is said to affirm that the British in return for military and economic assistance are intending to allow the United States clandestine use of the Carmine research and exploration stations for military—and, what's more, nuclear—purposes, that will represent a direct threat to the USSR. As I'm sure you appreciate, Canada has no alternative but to buy." He stood up and gave me a sad, sympathetic smile. "Now I must go to mass. At least you'll have a little time, *mon vieux.*"

But what was the use of time? I didn't need time to realize that the situation was desperate. All the charges against me and the Carmine Project had been combined and amplified into one great, overwhelming accusation, made in such circumstances and supported by such evidence that the majority of Canadians couldn't fail to believe it. Already

there had been rumours; I remembered the warnings I had
received from Gavin Brown's lawyer friend and Walter's
aunt. Now, unless it could be demonstrated that this document was a forgery, not only would I, the British Ambassador, become *persona non grata* but Canada would almost
certainly sever relations with Britain and the United States.
And the communists would be in an ideal position to see
that those relations were not renewed. Woods-Dawson's
fears, in fact, had all been justified.

"You were to show me the supposed proof of our nefar-
ious doings," I said to Paul, surprised by the calmness of
my own voice.

"Yes," he said. "First, the Xeroxed pages of the document, which are absolutely damning." He passed them across
the table to me.

"You mean they would be, if they weren't a fake." I took
them reluctantly, read them through and tossed them back
to him in disgust. "Any information as to how the document
is meant to have come into this chap's possession?"

"No."

"Have you asked him?"

"We've not had a chance. He sends us letters with instructions and we put notices in the paper to express agreement. So far that's been our only means of communication.
Tomorrow we'll indicate that we're prepared to buy."

"The President has definitely made up his mind, then?"

"In the circumstances what else can he do?"

I shrugged. "May I see the rest of the stuff."

"Of course." Paul hesitated. "Mark—I hate to remind
you of the liaison between your sister and Mr. Coller of the
Central Intelligence Agency. It's an important part of the
picture. Don't ignore it."

"I won't," I said evenly. I understood now why Paul had
said yesterday that this was "the worst possible moment"
for Coller's cover to be split wide open; no doubt the communists had picked it for that very reason. I glanced through
the "letters" which Paul had given me. "Are all these words
taken from Ottawa newspapers?"

"Yes, but that doesn't help. Incidentally there were no
fingerprints on anything, and nothing to identify the sender."

"I wouldn't have expected it. They're very thorough."

"The photographs are interesting."

I looked at the photographs of Coller and myself shaking hands as if to seal some bargain, of Coller with his arm around Melanie's shoulders, of Coller and Melanie and me in an earnest group. I stared at them with dawning comprehension. They had been taken at the Kings' lot during that snowmobiling party either by the man who had shot at us so skilfully or perhaps by a companion of his. The incident had served not only to link my name with Coller's in the news media but had also provided a chance to photograph us in seemingly suspicious circumstances; formerly meaningless, it now—like so many other things—made sense. I turned the prints over. Each was marked: Brit. Ambassador, Dr. L. and CIA man at top secret meeting in Gatineau.

"These weren't taken in the Gatineau," I said. "They were taken at Edgar's lot. I can show you the very place."

Paul nodded. "During that snowmobiling party? I guessed it. I recognized your clothes. And the others?"

"One is Coller leaving the Residence after our Christmas Eve party, to which we hadn't invited him. Edgar stole some invitation cards, you remember. The shadowy figure inside the hall is probably my houseman. It certainly isn't me." The photograph was labelled: CIA man, Coller, waves goodbye to Brit. Ambassador after meeting at Brit. Embassy. "As for the other two, I've no idea. It's me. It's Coller. Presumably it's Coller's Ottawa apartment, as it says. I wouldn't know. I've never been there. The photographs must've been faked somehow. Is that all?"

"These."

These were a couple of photostats. The first was of a crumpled memorandum that might have been salvaged from a wastepaperbasket. It read: "Re Carmine. Work proceeding too slowly. Impress Brits time of utmost importance if agreement . . ." The handwriting was said to be John Coller's. I didn't doubt that it was an excellent facsimile.

The second was a copy of what seemed to be the last page of a progress report on the Carmine Project. It was typed but had Coller's signature attached. There was also a postscript in his handwriting. "Lowrey assures me work is further advanced than this suggests."

I handed the photostats back to Paul and made a hopeless gesture. "What can I say—except to reiterate that none of this is true? The communists have conspired to sell your President a spurious document in circumstances that'll cause him to believe it to be authentic. By the grace of God— and thanks to your help and the President's perspicacity— I've had the chance to prove the existence of this conspiracy. And I would have thought that invalidated the document. Assuming that the President accepts my argument, I can't understand why he doesn't tell this chap and his phoney document to go to hell."

"That my dear Sir Mark, is because you over-simplify. What you don't understand are the convolutions of the communist mind."

"Excellence."

I hadn't heard the door open behind me but Paul was already on his feet. He drew back the chair at the head of the table and helped the President to seat himself. I stood and sat again as the old man gestured to me. He seemed to bring a faint smell of incense into the room. I wished I knew how good a Catholic and how much an anti-communist he was; on the answer could depend my chance of convincing him to reject the document. But I didn't understand the convolutions of *his* mind either; I should have remembered that primarily he was a politician.

Disconcertingly he said: "I do accept your argument, Sir Mark, but not your conclusion. I would like nothing better than to tell this chap and his phoney document to go to hell. I can assure you of that. But I suspect that that is precisely what the communists hope I will do. In fact I intend to buy it, as I said, and make it public. I haven't any choice."

"Make it public! You yourself would make it public?" I was aghast. "But, *Excellence,*" I protested, "surely that's preposterous? You're saying that, even though you believe it to be a forgery, you intend to publicize a document that's absolutely damning to Canada's friends and could have violent repercussions throughout the country. I must have misunderstood you."

But I hadn't misunderstood him. He intended to do just that and nothing I could say was going to stop him. He hadn't, he reiterated, any choice. The communists had him in a cleft stick. If he refused to buy or if he bought and kept the information secret, they would see to it that what he had done was known. The Carmine document would find its way to the news media anyhow, there would be an appalling outcry and not only would the Western Allies have gained nothing but his political enemies would have him ousted from the Presidency and replaced by some communist-backed character. On the other hand, he argued, if he stayed on the side of the apparent angels, he could use his great influence to support the Western Alliance and oppose the communists, thus negating the worst effects of the published document.

I saw his point but, if this was the best we could hope for, it was a grim outlook. "Supposing you were to repudiate the document and inform the Canadian people that they were being made the victims of a communist plot, *Excellence?*" I suggested tentatively. At once I knew I was asking too much. He was shaking his head violently. He neither could nor would play openly with the British. "I do have proof."

"In the present climate of opinion my people wouldn't believe it—not even if I swore to it myself. Many would, of course, but not the majority. And I am not a dictator, though I may sometimes seem to act like one. As for your proof, Sir Mark, what is it? The confession of a dead man, whose reputation, I'm sure, you wouldn't wish to malign. There is, alas, far more 'proof' against you and the Americans. No, what you suggest is impossible. It would split the country."

And to any Canadian politician this, I knew, was the ultimate sin. Nevertheless, I tried to argue but it was useless. The old man was adamant. It was obvious that we were going to have to play it his way or we would antagonize him and we couldn't afford that. We were wholly dependent on his good-will. The risks, however, were enormous.

Suddenly I was very angry and very afraid.

CHAPTER 6

January 4—January 5

IMMEDIATELY WE GOT back to the Residence I telephoned "Manchester" and the blonde voice answered. Mr. Dawson was with the Prime Minister. As soon as he returned from Downing Street he would telephone me. Yes, she understood that it was extremely urgent. Could she help? Just get hold of him as quickly as possible. Very well, she would arrange for a message to be left at Number 10.

Somewhat reassured, I put down the receiver and made myself a whisky and soda to remove the cloying taste of the Archbishop's sherry. I suppose that I ought to have set to at once and encoded a long telegram to London but the Office could wait, I had decided; it was only right that Woods-Dawson should be the first to know what was about to happen. Meanwhile the next thing for me was lunch.

I finished my drink and went along to join Gaby and Melanie and the temporary member of our family, Walter.

It was a dreary luncheon. Melanie was distrait, but made spasmodic efforts to be nice to Walter. Walter himself, embarrassed by their "engagement," was more silent than usual. Gaby was worrying about me and trying not to show it; driving home, I had given her the barest bones of what the President had told me. And I was on edge, yearning for the telephone to ring. We were all glad when the meal came to an end and we could go into the drawing-room for coffee.

Gaby had just poured my second cup when Woods-
Dawson telephoned.

He began at once by saying that he had been discussing
me with the Prime Minister. He had made Himself come
up from Chequers specifically for that purpose and Himself
hadn't objected; he could recognize a crisis when he saw
one, especially when a lot of his supporters had relations
in Canada and votes could be lost.

"My dear Mark," Woods-Dawson continued when I made
no response, "it's you we've been talking about, our man
in Ottawa—and the Canadian crisis. I'd have told you about
it earlier but you were praying to your God."

"Tell me about it now!" I said and was surprised at the
authority in my own voice.

"Of course, dear boy." Suddenly he sounded grim and
businesslike. "It's dire—I've heard—the source is absolutely reliable—that in the very near future public opinion
against us and the Americans is going to be whipped up to
a record-breaking high, until it'll be unpatriotic for any
Canadian not to cry: "To hell with the bastards!" And when
the cry goes up the means to send us on our way will be
available—guns, bombs, gas, whatever should prove necessary. Then Canada will have new friends and new allies
and, in a short time will become a communist-dominated
country. At least that's the theory of the thing."

"Yes," I said. "It fits."

"What?" I had actually surprised Woods-Dawson.

"I know what's to trigger it off," I said and told him
about the forged document as succinctly as I could, doing
my best to answer his explosive questions and ignoring his
scathing comments.

Eventually a gusty sigh breathed along the transatlantic
cable. "Christ!" he said. "The communists have been clever,
unbelievably clever. Whoever organized this one's a genius.
We've been completely outwitted. Poor old Mark! You know,
dear boy, in the circumstances you really haven't done at
all badly."

"Thanks," I said, my voice heavy with sarcasm. "It's a
pity that's an obituary notice."

He didn't answer. There was a long silence. Then he

said: "Well, it's more than one can say for the brilliant John Coller of the Central Intelligence Agency, isn't it? He could scarcely have done worse had he tried. You know, nobody would ever believe he and that brainy political scientist sister of yours could've been such bloody fools."

It must have been about now that the germ of an idea came to him for suddenly and abruptly he ended our conversation and said goodbye, promising to be in touch very soon. It was a moment or two before I could bring myself to put down the receiver, even though my link with him was already snapped. I felt unutterably low. I even wondered if he would bother to telephone me as he had promised, which was grossly unfair; Nanny had never let me down yet.

He telephoned about four hours later. In the interval I had kept myself busy making plans to safeguard British lives and property if it became necessary—not to mention such important things as secret files—and drafting an enormous telegram to London explaining the President's proposition; this Woods-Dawson had told me not to send until the following day. As I picked up the receiver I saw that it had begun to snow again.

I listened to what Woods-Dawson had to say, at first dully and then in utter astonishment. I was dumbfounded. "Are you mad?" I asked, in all seriousness. There was a long tirade from the other side of the Atlantic. "But we can't do it!" I said firmly. "It's completely immoral."

He laughed without humour. "Don't be so naïve! If we don't do it God knows what will happen in Canada. Whatever the President may say about his great influence, once this Carmine document becomes public property he won't have a hope in heaven of controlling events. This whole thing has been too well organized."

"Nevertheless, to make John Coller—"

"And it'll be a bloody business, bloodier than the communists expect. There could even be civil war. A lot of Canadians will fight rather than be dominated by the Reds and the Americans will back them if we don't. Canada could become a battlefield. Do you want to be responsible for that, Mark?"

"Your plan's not even practical."

"That's better. Forget your middle-class morality and concentrate on how it's to be done."

"You mean how I'm to do it."

"Are you scared, dear boy?"

"Yes, I'm scared. Who wouldn't be, nannied by a madman like you?"

"Of course, you'll need assistance other than your house staff for the fiddling work," he said thoughtfully. "There's any amount to do before tomorrow. Alex Stocker's the obvious one except that . . ."

"No!"

"Why not?"

I had spoken instinctively but I could give a reasoned answer. "I don't trust him and I doubt his competence. If he discovered his wife and Coller were lovers he might blow everything. He's devoted to her."

This was the point at which I was hooked, though I didn't realize it at the time. I went on arguing with Woods-Dawson or I thought I was arguing. In fact what I was doing was acting as a sounding board to help him crystallize his ideas. But I continued to protest.

"It won't work," I said desperately. "And the Americans'll never forgive us for trying it."

"Never forgive *you*, you mean. Unfortunate Ambassador, under pressure for months, perhaps a mistake, too inexperienced, too young—but all very difficult in the circumstances. You know the line the Office will take and the Americans will play. They'll be in no position to alienate us."

I said nothing.

"Mark, there's an even possibility that the plan will work. If it does the reward will be enormous. The communists will have wasted months on an operation which we'll have completely scotched. The President will be our friend. The Carmine Project will go ahead. And there'll be no riots, no bloodshed. You know, if you don't take the chance you'll never be able to look yourself in the face again."

And if I did take it—as I knew I was going to—would I be able to look myself in the face then?

Gaby thought not.

I found her in the drawing-room where the houseman was laying out the pre-dinner drinks. Melanie, pleading a headache, had gone to lie down. I told Gaby what I was planning to do and she just looked at me. I hadn't expected her to like it—God knows I didn't like it myself—but Woods-Dawson had persuaded me that it was the lesser evil. Now, for my own sake, I had to persuade Gaby and she wasn't easy to persuade. I succeeded only after a long and bitter argument.

Oddly enough this hardened my resolve to go through with it. The alternative, as outlined to Gaby, seemed more and more appalling. I had to try to prevent it, by whatever means. Not that I expected to succeed. But I was going to do my utmost.

Determined, I went up to Melanie's room. My sister was lying on the bed with a book beside her but she hadn't been reading. She looked at me resentfully. Her eyes were red.

"What do you want?"

"Anything John Coller gave you. A letter, a card, a present—anything with his writing on it. I don't really know."

"For God's sake—why?"

I told her and prepared for another argument. But my sister was a pragmatist. She didn't argue. She listened quite calmly, then got off the bed and started rummaging in her chest-of-drawers. She produced a pair of scarlet boots appliquéd with flowers, which I had been Coller buying in *The Canada Goose,* a poem either original or copied but signed by him and—what was to prove invaluable—some photographs of the two of them, singly and together.

I was now almost fully equipped for the first stage of this unholy enterprise.

I watched the blood from my finger mingle with the water, swirl around the wash-basin and gurgle down the drain. It was a deep cut which wouldn't stop bleeding. I cursed under my breath. By now, three o'clock on Monday morning, I was tired and edgy.

I had been careless and let the splicer slip. Failure seemed

inevitable. I hadn't realized how difficult it was to edit a
tape skilfully. In spite of the effort I had sweated into the
thing, the end-product was still self-evidently phoney. There
were too many bumps at the splices, false intonations, blurring of sound in the wrong places. I was tempted to abandon
the whole idea. And yet a tape of Edgar's conversation with
Walter, if only I could doctor it properly, would be of ines-
timable value. It would do much to support the letters.

The letters were ready. Paul Brill had the original of
Edgar's written confession but I had a photostat. I also had
a long screed that Edgar had sent Gaby before we came to
Ottawa, containing advice and instructions about the sort
of things we should bring with us. Between them they provided a fine example of Edgar's ultra-small, neat handwriting. And I had a natural talent for forgery, which I had
perfected during many misspent hours at school—something Woods-Dawson had not forgotten. Now, for the first
time, I was using it for real.

In fact the contents of the letters had presented more
difficulty than the forgery. Some discrepancy could always
be put down to Edgar's distraught state. The wording, however, had to be perfect for my purpose.

When I got back to the study I read them through again.

Dear Mark,
    This will be a shock to you and I can't go into
details now. Walter will fill you in. He knows the
whole story. But I'm writing to you in case he decides
not to tell you because you're a Brit. I owe you the
truth which is, briefly, that I've been blackmailed into
helping set you up for that bastard Coller and his
stinking communist pals. Forgive me if you can. I'm
truly sorry. Goodbye.
                                Edgar.

That one was satisfactory, I decided. It would allow me
to contact Walter in the event that he didn't first contact
me, as I hoped he would, and it would ensure that he
couldn't avoid telling me about Edgar's letter to him, which
had been much tricker to compose.

Dear Walter,
[I read, trying to put myself in Walter's place:]
    The authorities will find me out at the lot. I'm sure
this is best for me and everyone, including the Department. I know you'll do what you can for the kids
and Heather. Fortunately my insurance covers suicide.
Two other things. Please tell Mark everything. He has
a right to know. And, if you haven't already, warn
our people about John Coller. The stuff on the radio
about him being in CIA is a lot of balls—unless he's
a double agent. Coller is a communist. I can't give
you proof but I'm not guessing. I know. I have good
reason to know. Sorry for being so much trouble.
Goodbye.

                        Edgar.

    That too was satisfactory—satisfactory enough, I hoped,
to convince the President that poor bloody Coller might well
be a communist. Because John Coller of the Central Intelligence Agency, Coller the professional, was to become
Coller the scapegoat—if I could succeed in carrying out
Woods-Dawson's plan. But I didn't want to think about
Coller as a person.
    I continued work on the tape and now things seemed to
go right. I wasn't trying to fabricate conversation between
Walter and Edgar but to edit what I already had. By cun-
ningly repeating or interpolating phrases and putting sen-
tences out of context I finally managed to achieve some
passages which, though not so damning by themselves that
Walter on hearing them on a re-recorded tape would reject
them, were nevertheless a bitter confirmation of the letters.
And when I had also made sure that there was nothing to
contradict the impression that I wanted to make I gave up.
Technically my effort was still not perfect but it was the
best I could do. And I was almost beyond caring.
    Melanie came in with a tray of early breakfast and while
we buttered toast and drank yet more coffee—we had con-
sumed gallons during the night—I played her the final version. She and Gaby had been an enormous help to me as

Woods-Dawson, after I had turned down his suggestion of
Alex Stocker, had suggested that they might. Indeed my
sister had made up, at least in part, for the madness which
had helped to land us in this mess. She had made some
bright suggestions about the tape and the letters. She had
spent hours, with Gaby's help, finding and cutting out from
old Ottawa newspapers the sort of words used in the messages that the President had received. She had pasted up
most of a supposedly new message and she had composed
from the words in the poem Coller had given her a somewhat
peculiar note, which I copied in his handwriting but later
decided to abandon. Above all, she had given me moral
support, if that wasn't the wrong phrase for such an immoral
undertaking.

"That's fine," she said of the tape. "Now all that's left
is a little photography."

"Yes. I'd better go and put on the right suit."

"And shave. Have you seen yourself? You look like the
wrath of God."

"What a kind, sisterly remark," I said and gave her a
kiss. "Thanks."

I went upstairs slowly, thinking about the photographs.
Woods-Dawson had warned me not to use the copies which
the President had provided for me as they were probably
marked; but Melanie had had another crop. These were of
herself and John Coller, and had been taken by Coller's own
camera, a polaroid such as Melanie and thousands of others
owned. At least three of them could have been sent to the
President to prove what chums Coller and Melanie were
and one of Coller alone showed him dressed as he had been
in a couple of the faked photographs. It only remained to
provide a few of me as I had appeared in these same fakes.
Then Coller would never be able to talk his way out of their
possession.

In the bedroom Gaby was fast asleep, exhausted. I had
insisted she should go to bed; she hadn't Melanie's stamina—or her stomach for this rotten business. Now as I
moved around the room, quietly undressing, she didn't stir.
I went into the bathroom and showered and shaved, which
gave me a temporary lift. Then I put on the suit, tie, shirt,

socks and shoes that appeared in the photograph, checking every detail. I was ready for the photographic session.

I had expected to be finished with this in half an hour but I had been over-optimistic. The camera was pretty well foolproof but by now Melanie and I were tired to a point of extreme irritability. Moreover, there were technical details, lighting and background for example, which made the reproduction that I wanted to achieve far from easy. By the time we had overcome these difficulties and Melanie was again managing to hold the camera straight I was so wooden-looking that that wouldn't do. And we struggled on.

Eventually we succeeded, but too late for me to slip into bed beside Gaby and have a reasonable sleep as I had hoped. So I sent Melanie off to bed and, after another long session with Woods-Dawson, settled for the armchair.

CHAPTER 7

January 5

AFTER AN HOUR or so's cat-nap I ordered the Rolls and was driven to the Chancery. The snow had stopped—another eight inches had fallen during the night—and the ploughs had managed to clear the main roads; but the side roads were clogged and traffic moved slowly. A cheerful voice on the radio announced that the violence of the weekend storm had dislocated life throughout Ontario and Quebec. In Ottawa power lines were down, some telephones weren't working, no morning papers had been delivered, mail deliveries were uncertain, the airport was closed, taxis were unobtainable, public transport—never very satisfactory—was struggling hopelessly to deal with the unusual influx of passengers, who were either unable or unwilling to put their own cars at risk, and hundreds of people were going to be late for work. I flicked the radio knob irritably and the bright voice faded.

None of this was going to help. My plans could depend upon the normality of transport and communications. Unexpected delays could make a mess of everything. I caught myself biting my lip and forced myself to relax. It was no use worrying about what might happen; that way lay panic. I must deal with each problem as it arose, efficiently and methodically—and God help the general strategy.

The beautifully-kept Rolls, with its fluttering Union Jack and its *corps diplomatique* plates adding to its prestige, drew

up in front of the Chancery. The uniformed chauffeur opened
the door and saluted as the British Ambassador descended
from the car.

"I should think it'll be within the hour. Keep yourself
ready."

"Yes, Sir Mark. Very good."

No passer-by would have believed, I thought wryly as I
went through the plate-glass doors which the security guard
was holding open for me, that he had just seen two men
making the final arrangement for a burglary. I didn't really
believe it myself. My thoughts switched abruptly to my
houseman. At least what he was doing wasn't illegal—or
was it? Could he be charged with entering a government
building under false pretences with intent to commit a felony? Surely delivering a forged letter couldn't be described
as a felony. Perhaps it was a misdemeanour. Certainly if he
was caught with the letter on him it would put paid to the
rest of my scheming. If only I knew how he was getting
on.

But it was the best part of an hour before he arrived and
by then I was well dug into my in-tray, just as if it were a
normal morning. I wanted it to appear a normal morning.
When my secretary brought him in I managed to finish the
telegram I was reading before I looked up. I had to swallow
my surprise. He was wearing a long black coat with a fake
fur collar and a fake fur hat to match, so that he seemed
taller than he was. Horn-rimmed glasses, tinted against the
glare of the snow, hid his eyes and a briefcase completed
his disguise. He could have been any foreign service officer
on a winter's day in Ottawa.

"Well?" I hadn't meant to snap.

"Satisfactory, Sir Mark."

"Good!" I gestured towards a chair. "You had no trouble?"

"About the letter, no. It was a piece of cake. I waited
until there was a steady stream going into the Department,
walked past the guard who barely glanced at my pass and
took the lift up to the floor above Mr. Walter Eland. I left
my hat and coat in the gents, took the stairs down and
sauntered along the corridor until I came to Mr. Eland's

office. I gave the letter to his secretary, said it had been left with "us" by mistake and she said, "Thanks, I was just going to take Mr. Eland's mail in to him." No questions. And I went the same way I'd come. Their security's something awful."

"Yes," I said weakly, envying him his insouciance. "That's splendid."

"The only dicey moment was when Mr. Eland opened the door of his room and I thought he was coming out."

"Did he see you? Would he have asked his secretary who you were, what you wanted?" I was suddenly anxious.

"Not a chance, Sir Mark. He had papers in his hand and things on his mind. He went back into his room and shut the door."

My anxiety faded and I faced the fact that really it had been hope. If Walter so much as questioned the source of the letter, my ploy, Woods-Dawson's ploy, the British ploy became suspect. And I wouldn't have to break into John Coller's flat! Despising myself, I said: "What about Cook? How did she get on?"

He ignored the incongruity in the circumstances of calling his wife Cook. "Not so well, Sir Mark. I dropped her at the General Post Office in Confederation Square as arranged and picked her up again. But her telephone calls weren't fruitful. She couldn't trace Mr. Coller."

"You mean he's not at his Embassy?"

"No—and there's no answer at his flat. His secretary said he had gone to Montreal for the weekend. She wasn't very forthcoming but, when pressed, she said that he had gone by air and, since all flights in and out of Ottawa are cancelled because of the storm, she didn't expect him back until tomorrow or even the day after. She positively refused to give an address or a phone number for him."

"I see." Coller had told Melanie that he was going to Montreal so this fitted. "We'll have to assume he's still there then. I'd rather have had him pinpointed but it can't be helped."

The buzzer on my intercom sounded and I pressed down the switch. My secretary's voice said: "Mr. Walter Eland would like to speak to you on the telephone, Sir Mark."

"Tell him I'm in conference," I said. "And when he rings again say I went out before you could give me his message."

"Very good, Sir Mark."

I turned back to the houseman and he gave me a sympathetic smile. "It's working," he said. It was a statement.

"Yes," I agreed, taken off guard; I wasn't usually so transparent. "It's working. So I had better be about my business."

He nodded. "Good luck!" he said.

"Thanks," I said, absurdly pleased by the fact that he had spoken as one equal to another.

Because I wasn't his equal. This was brought home to me some fifteen minutes later as I waited in the Rolls for my chauffeur to decide when we should act. The palms of my hands were damp with sweat, my lips dry, my collar constricting and my whole body taut. I yearned for his calm self-assurance. And I wished myself anywhere else but where I was—some fifty yards from the entrance to the block of apartments where John Coller lived.

"Now, I think, Sir Mark!"

A jalopy had drawn up across the road and disgorged two girls, students by the look of them from Carleton or Ottawa U., carrying books. At the same time a lady, covered from head to foot in furs, decided that her large grey poodle had had enough of the great outdoors. We all converged on the apartment block at the same time.

The doorman hurried from the office where he had been having coffee and flung open the inner door for the poodle, whom he addressed by name. The lady answered for her dog. The students followed her, one of them spilling her pile of books. And in the blessed confusion we made our non-memorable entrance, the doorman being far too occupied to ask us whom we wished to see.

We went up in the high-speed elevator—floors ten and above—with the lady and the poodle. The poodle sniffed at me suspiciously; perhaps he sensed my nervousness. She pulled him away and smiled her apologies when he persisted. I smiled back. Fortunately the Muzak was turned up high and the mindless music which flooded the lift prevented conversation. They got out first.

We continued to the next floor where John Coller had his flat. I pressed his buzzer and waited. I tried again. There was still no answer. The corridor was deserted. It suddenly occurred to me how surprised I would have been if Coller had opened his own front door. I hadn't the faintest idea what I should have said to him.

"There's not too much time, Sir Mark. Somebody's sure to come."

"Go ahead then."

I stood between my chauffeur and the lifts, praying that nobody would come out of one of the flats while he was diddling the lock. Time stretched. I listened to him muttering under his breath and to the delicate chink of metal on metal. Then I heard the hum of a lift, the whoosh of opening doors. In two strides we were across the corridor, presumably waiting to be admitted by whoever lived opposite. But the man turned away from us without giving us a glance and let himself into the nearest flat.

We turned to Coller's lock, which almost immediately produced a satisfactory click. The door yielded. I put out my hand to swing it open and a strident voice called:

"Mr. Coller's away for a long weekend."

I turned slowly. The young woman was waiting for a lift to take her down to the laundry room because she had a basket piled high with dirty clothes which she clutched to her middle. Below the basket were a pair of jeans and sandals, above it a red T-shirt, a pointed face and two bright, observant eyes. She began to walk towards us. She couldn't fail to notice that Coller's door was ajar. I froze.

"Mister Kola? A-ach, madame—we have the incorrect floor! We must go higher. We want apartment ten but not on twelfth floor."

My chauffeur hurried to meet her, eager, self-apologetic, blocking her view of the door and me. He had left his cap in the car and he was a man in some sort of dark blue uniform under a raincoat, a foreigner to judge by his Central European accent. I hovered in the background while he elaborated his explanation, holding her attention until the lift came and we were rid of her. But as soon as she had coped with her laundry she would be back; she mustn't find either of us in this corridor again.

We slid into John Coller's flat and I, for one, felt an enormous sense of anti-climax. All this might seem hilarious in a year's time but at the moment I had lost my sense of humour. That so much could depend on some casual co-incidence wasn't in the least funny; it was awe-inspiring.

"Gloves!" snapped my chauffeur.

"Sorry," I apologized and felt in my coat pocket for the thin gloves he had provided.

"You must hurry, Sir Mark," he said.

I didn't apologize again. I thrust my hands into the gloves, swearing softly when the fingers weren't quite long enough for me and went to look around the flat, which was an exact mirror-image of Walter's. There was a hall with a walk-in storage cupboard, a passage with more cupboards, kitchen, bathroom, bedroom and the large L-shaped room for living and dining. It was furnished pleasantly enough in a bright, modern fashion with gay prints on the white walls but some-how I didn't associate it with John Coller—or anyone else; it was as impersonal as a hotel suite. Yet, for all I knew, it was just the job for a happy American bachelor in CIA.

My inspection was perfunctory. I hadn't come to steal or to snoop. I was looking for the most valid places in which to plant the photographs and newspapers, and the unfinished messages that Gaby and Melanie had spent so much of the night preparing. I had already given the matter some thought and Woods-Dawson had made suggestions. Now I had a stroke of luck.

I found, together with the polaroid camera Melanie had told me that Coller possessed and a very expensive Zeiss, a box of photographs. I rifed through them. He seemed to like taking people. They were all of people; people skiing, snowmobiling, playing tennis, swimming, people sitting, standing, walking, talking, people alone and people to-gether. Among the people whom I recognized were Melanie and Sally Stocker, but they were in admirable company, which included the wives of two Cabinet Ministers. This was the perfect place to put the photographs I had brought with me.

The other things were more of a problem. I had hoped to find a pile of newspapers to which I could add the doctored ones but there wasn't a newspaper in the flat, only magazines. In the end I put the cut newspapers with a few loose words in a suitcase, locked it—the key had been left in a pocket—and put it in the back of a cupboard. There was no danger that the newspapers wouldn't be found; the CFP would rip the flat apart—if all went according to plan.

I hurried along the passage to the hall. Finding the key to the suitcase had given me a bright idea. I knew what I wanted to do with the half-finished messages, cut-out words, paper and gum. I stopped abruptly as my chauffeur held up a commanding hand.

"Cleaning women," he mouthed.

He was peering through the one-way glass which enabled him to see a small area directly in front of the door, where the women must have been standing. I could hear their voices clearly.

". . . must do number ten."

"What for? E's away for the weekend, you said."

"So 'e'll be back today then. I'll just give it a dust-round and make it nice for 'im."

"You and your Mr. Coller. You've got a thing about 'im."

"What if I 'ave?"

"Oh, come on, Kath. Let's go and 'ave our cawfee."

"Okay," Kath agreed reluctantly.

I expelled my breath slowly. I was shaken but not as badly as before. Either I was getting hardened or the fact that I had been actually doing something had steadied me. The women's voice receded along the corridor; the comic character episode was ended.

"I'm almost finished," I said. "I want you to lock a drawer."

"To *lock* it?"

I led the way to the desk. I had tried the drawers. They were all unlocked and contained nothing personal; Coller, I thought, must have kept his private papers in his office. I cleared the bottom drawer and put in it the paper, glue, scissors, bits of newspaper and the half-completed messages. I was now counting on the flat being searched before

Coller got back from Montreal tomorrow.

"Lock it," I said, "and let's get out of here."

I suppose we had had our quota of alarms and excursions because our departure from Coller's flat and from the apartment block was without incident. I sat in the back of the Rolls, once more the British Ambassador, and hugged myself in relief and thanksgiving. The expedition had been a success; the evidence to prove John Coller a communist had been planted in his flat. Moreover, I had been right to insist on doing it myself. It had been worth the risk. I understood better than anyone the scene that had had to be set and, if any error had been made, I was the one who might have the chance later to adapt the scenario. At the moment all was going well.

This was confirmed when I got back to the Chancery; Walter had telephoned twice more. I brushed aside Alex Stocker, who wanted to talk about a party of our MPs eager for a free junket to Canada and the Arctic, and my Trade Commissioner who wanted to talk about all the complaints he had received on the servicing of some stuff we had sold to the Government of Ontario. I left them grumbling to each other and asked my secretary to get Walter on the phone.

"Mark, I must see you."

"Yes—of course."

"At once."

"Well, I'm pretty busy at the..."

"Mark, please. Did you get a letter this morning?"

"My dear chap, a pile of them and telegrams and God knows what else. You should see my in-tray." I sounded acid.

Walter made the sort of remark that one does *not* make to an ambassador to one's country. And I grinned broadly. He had taken the bait. I agreed to meet him—as soon as we could both get there—at the Residence where, as I had every reason to know, a letter from Edgar would indeed be waiting. Phase two had begun.

I let Walter make the running. He proved more gullible than I had expected, though I'm sure that in his place I wouldn't have been any more perceptive, and seemed to accept everything at its face value. He did give me one nasty moment when he queried the tape, saying he couldn't remember Edgar being so explicit about Coller. But he blamed his own memory; what else could he do? Even if the idea had crossed his mind it wasn't credible that I should have fiddled the recording. And there were the letters.

As Walter said, there was no question about it. John Coller was a communist agent. Edgar had made a definite accusation. And why should Edgar lie when he was about to take his own life?

I nodded soberly. (It was an argument I hadn't overlooked.) For Walter's benefit I had tried to run the gamut of the emotions, astonishment, ridicule, doubt—finally conviction; the CIA man was in fact a communist! I felt like some ham in a fifth-rate repertory company. Lack of sleep was beginning to catch up with me. But Walter, I reminded myself, was the easiest of the three I had to dupe—neither Paul Brill nor the President would be so trustful—and I was only half way through with Walter.

"I'll need to take the tape, Mark, and the two letters. And do I have your permission to say we agreed for the family's sake not to leave the suicide note by Edgar's body?"

My permission! His civility made me cringe inside. "No," I said.

"No? What do you mean? No to what?" he asked mildly.

"No to the tape. You may have a copy of Edgar's letter to me but only in return for a copy of his letter to you. As for the suicide note, I don't mind."

He just stared at me. "Why?"

"Will you have a drink?"

"Thank you."

Neither of us spoke while I poured our whiskies. God knows what Walter was thinking. I came and sat in an armchair opposite him and sipped my drink. And an irrational fear struck me that the study hadn't been cleaned; Walter could notice a forgotten piece of tape or some fragment of newspaper lying on the floor and everything would be ruined. I forced myself to smile at him.

"I'm sorry," I said, "but there are things you don't know, Walter."

"What things?" he asked bluntly, pulling at his moustache. He didn't return my smile.

I pretended to hesitate. Then I said: "Yesterday I had an interview with your President. I shouldn't tell you what was discussed but in the circumstances..." I made it as brief as possible but left nothing out. "So you can appreciate how serious the situation is. Nevertheless, the communists have been so bloody clever there's nothing either your people or mine can do about it. I've been up most of the night talking to London and my brief is to watch and pray, but nobody's hopeful there. In a few weeks our countries will almost certainly have severed relations with each other and you and I will be on opposite sides. In fact, I expect to be recalled by the Office with due opprobrium. Therefore, dear Walter, I'm hanging on to that tape and Edgar's letter. I'm not quite sure why, but they might come in useful."

"But surely—" Walter began and stopped.

"What?" I prompted, willing him to say what I wanted him to say.

"But surely the fact that Coller's a communist makes all the difference. It completely negates the supporting evidence that the enemy has built up so carefully and invalidates this Carmine document before it has even been seen." He spoke slowly as his mind searched for snags. When I remained silent, he frowned. "Of course, you didn't need me to tell you that. You're afraid the Canadians won't take action. That's it, isn't it?"

"Yes. The thing's political dynamite. I don't believe the President'll touch Coller unless there's irrefutable proof. As I see it, Walter, if Edgar's confession isn't enough to make the President denounce the communist plot, Edgar's accusation by itself won't be enough to make him publicly condemn Coller."

"But he must do something, Mark. The CFP can look for proof, search Coller's apartment, tap his phone—I don't know."

"There isn't much time."

"Then I suggest we try to get hold of Paul Brill immediately. For God's sake, man, think what's at stake."

I grinned weakly, apologized and reminded him how tired I was. That at least was true. I could so easily have gone to sleep in the big, comfortable armchair, except that I couldn't relax until Paul Brill had been located.

By the time Paul had come and gone I was feeling better. I was actually hopeful. Walter had been splendid, taking on himself the full burden of explanation so that I was a mere supernumerary—just what I wanted to seem. It had been too easy; Paul had accepted the letters and the tape without question. In fact everything so far had been much simpler than I had expected. I could only assume this was because I had a guilty conscience about the unfortunate John Coller; I thrust that thought away from me.

I got rid of Walter and telephoned Woods-Dawson, who was reasonably satisfied with the way things were going. But we had a short, sharp argument on the subject of Alex Stocker. Woods-Dawson had suddenly announced that I was to tell Alex the whole story of the communist conspiracy and its outcome to date. This really annoyed me. I would have been glad of Alex's support in the beginning but I had had strict orders not to confide in him which hadn't helped our relationship; now, when I was sure he was neither dependable nor trustworthy, my lords and masters had decided on a complete *volte face*. It was infuriating. I protested vehemently, wasting my breath.

"No use kicking, dear boy," Woods-Dawson said. "The instruction comes from Himself direct. He believes Stocker should be briefed in the event that he's to take over from you."

"In the event that—? God rot all politicians!" I said banging down the receiver and cutting short Woods-Dawson's laughter.

Then I went to bed. Gaby and Melanie were out for lunch and I was able to sleep, undisturbed, for almost two hours. I could have done with another ten.

The waiting was going to be dreadful. But there was nothing else to do except wait, wait for the President to make up his mind. Walter and I were available if he should wish to see us; Paul didn't seem to think this likely, not at the moment. And I appreciated that the decision would be a political one.

Nevertheless, I was fairly confident that the old man

would act and the first thing would be a search of John Coller's flat. With Coller safely in Montreal, as they would easily discover, they had nothing to lose. It had to happen that way, I argued to myself. They would search the flat, find the stuff I had planted and arrest the wretched Coller on his return. There would be a fine scandal but not the kind the communists had planned. And the end would justify the means. Or was this wishful thinking?

I had an early cup of tea and went back to the Chancery. There was plenty to do there. I read the telegrams, dictated a couple of memos, blue-pencilled a speech which someone had written for me, and saw the Trade Commissioner and the Security Officer. I balked, however, at considering arrangements for my projected visit to the Carmine Project.

It was after six when I remembered Alex Stocker. I put out my hand to the intercom but I had sent my secretary home early because of the storm, and, though I could have used the internal telephone, on an impulse I went down the passage to Alex's rooms. His secretary had left too but there was a light under his door.

I knocked and went in. He was locking up and didn't look too pleased to see me.

"I've just rung Sally to say I'm on my way," he said ungraciously.

"I'm sorry. I won't keep you long."

"If it's about those MPs, can't it wait till morning?"

"It's not—and it can't wait."

"Very well." He sat down behind his desk, resigned. "We're dining with the German Ambassador."

"You'll have time to put on your black tie," I said coldly. "Meanwhile perhaps you'll be good enough to listen. It is important."

He flushed but didn't answer and, having impressed on him the need for complete secrecy—I specifically mentioned Sally, which didn't please him—I launched into my story. As I talked it occurred to me that I had been spending a great deal of time recently giving various versions of the communist conspiracy to various people. I made Alex's version as short as possible and strictly factual, cutting out all embroidery. He heard me through in almost total silence and interrupted only once.

"You mean you knew about this conspiracy before you came to Ottawa? And you never told me anything about it?"

"I only knew that there was a conspiracy. No details. Nothing about Carmine. And my instructions were to tell no one."

"I see." But obviously he didn't. He believed it had been my personal decision to keep him out of it and he resented that.

I sighed. "Shall I go on?"

"Please."

"This morning both Walter Eland and I received letters from Edgar King in which he stated that John Coller was in fact a communist..."

I gave it to him straight because I wanted to see his reactions. I hadn't any intention of deceiving him. And his reactions were predictable, amazed disbelief followed by amazed relief.

"My God," he said. "If Coller's a communist all the supporting evidence for this Carmine document breaks down and it's self-apparent that the chap who's trying to sell it is a phoney—a communist himself. We're saved, then."

"Assuming the President's prepared to act against Coller. Brill promised to let me know."

"Of course he will. We'll force him."

"It's not quite as simple as that. You see..."

And I was about to tell Alex the truth about the letters and the tape and the stuff planted in Coller's flat but he stood up, interrupting me.

"In fact the crisis is over. Now I understand why you've had permission to inform me about this conspiracy. I'm needed to help with the mopping up, I suppose. Well, as I said before, Mark, when I told you about seeing Coller and Melanie together, you can count on me—but not tonight, please. Sally will be furious if I'm late. So if you'll excuse me. You do understand, don't you?" Suddenly he grinned hugely. "The idea of your right-wing sister consorting with commie Coller has its amusing side, you must admit."

I was tired and worried and I wasn't going to let him get

away with that crack. I said: "Incidentally there's one thing you can tell Sally. Melanie has just become engaged to Walter Eland. Gaby'll be telephoning about a party for them very soon." Then brushing aside his surprised bumblings I wished him good-night and left him to go home.

I wonder sometimes what would have happened if I had told Alex that John Coller had been framed—by me, and that Melanie's engagement to Walter was strictly *de convenance*. It gives me nightmares.

CHAPTER 8

January 6—January 7

I HAD KNOWN the waiting was going to be rough, but not how rough. Time crawled, jumped, somersaulted and was almost back where it had started. The wear and tear on my nervous system was frightful.

Yesterday, although it had been understood that I was available, the President had expressed no wish to see me. But in the evening he sent for Walter and cross-questioned him for more than an hour, leaving Walter puzzled and upset and me little the wiser. Later, however, much later Paul had telephoned to say that the President had decided to take action of "a noncommittal kind," which wasn't nearly as discouraging as it sounded.

It meant—or so I had assumed—that a thorough search of Coller's flat would be made by the CFP during the night, before he got back from Montreal. Walter had urged the need for such a search and said that Paul had seemed to accept it as an obvious step. I had also assumed that, as a result of the search, I would hear this morning that undeniable proof of Coller's guilt had been found and even that he had already been arrested. But so far I hadn't heard a thing.

By midday I was really worried, sure that something had gone wrong or Paul would have been eager to contact me. But there was nothing I could do, except struggle along until it was time to meet him, as arranged, at the funeral parlour where Edgar King's friends and colleagues were paying their last respects before the body was flown to Toronto for interment. It was a bizarre but non-compromising meeting-place and, in the circumstances, peculiarly ironical. I couldn't help wondering if the memorial service in Edgar's honour, scheduled for late next week, would ever take place. If it did, it now seemed highly improbable that I would be present.

Not knowing what to expect, I arrived at the funeral parlour with Gaby shortly before three o'clock; Melanie had refused to attend what she called "a barbaric rite." We were greeted in the hall by one unctuous character and passed on to his twin, who was standing guard at the door which bore the name of Mr. Edgar King. From behind him came a steady murmur of voices, reasonably subdued—unlike the happy wake that was taking place further down the passage—and a strong smell of lilies which must have originated from an aerosol spray as I never saw a lily anywhere in the place.

"Will you sign the Book of Remembrance, please, sir."

I signed for myself and Gaby, ignoring the space for comments. I couldn't bring myself to write: "A dear friend and colleague" or "The Lowreys will miss him." What I wanted to write was "I forgive you. I hope you can forgive me;" but I didn't think his family would appreciate that.

A quick glance round the room as we were announced informed me that Paul hadn't arrived yet. I shook hands with Heather, who was grey-faced and drawn, and offered my condolences to Edgar's three teenage children, his blimpish father, Brigadier King, his brother who was a lawyer and his unmarried sister. Edgar's mother was under sedation, too shocked to travel to Ottawa. I refused to think what I had done, and was doing, to all these people. I went and stood by Edgar's closed coffin, my head bowed, until an oily voice announced Mr. and Mrs. Paul Brill. Then, as soon as possible, I cut Paul off from Lucille and the rest of the mourners.

"Can we talk here?" I asked.

"Briefly," he said. "I'm to tell you that we now have much more evidence against him. His apartment was searched

last night. The CFP found Ottawa newspapers with words
cut out, photographs of you and your sister, notes on the
Carmine Project, all sorts of stuff."   .

"Good God!" I said. "That's conclusive enough. Surely
he was very careless?"

Paul Brill shrugged. "Cocksure more likely. Who would
have suspected the CIA man?"

"At least we know now," I said, assuming complete confidence. "And that's splendid! It puts paid to this Carmine
document and the whole communist operation, doesn't it?"

"Mark—" Paul hesitated. "I'm afraid there are one or
two snags. First of all, John Coller has disappeared."

"Dis—disappeared?"

"Well, nobody knows where he is, not even his Embassy. They say he went to Montreal on Friday for the
weekend. He was expected back yesterday but the planes
were grounded because of the storm and he phoned to say
he was staying over for a day or two."

"But they must have an address or telephone number,"
I protested. "It's standard procedure. His Embassy's putting
up a smoke screen."

"No, I don't think so." Paul shook his head. "I was there
when the US Ambassador called. He said Coller was in a
privileged position. He half admitted he was in CIA. Seemingly, if Coller doesn't volunteer the information, people
don't ask where he's going or what he's doing."

"How nice for him," I said. "It must have made things
easy."

"But for what? That brings us to the second snag," Paul
said reluctantly. "The Ambassador swears that Coller's not
a communist. He pointed out that the stuff we discovered
in Coller's apartment could easily have been planted there
and that, apart from it, we've only Edgar's word. Edgar
could have been mistaken."

"That sounds possible but not highly probable," I said.
"What do you propose to do about it?"

Paul looked embarrassed. "The Ambassador was very
persuasive. We've agreed to find Coller unofficially and ask
him to explain—if he can. Until then we take no further
action."

"I see," I said bleakly.

This was a blow. Questions crowded into my mind but there was no point in asking them, at any rate of Paul. Paul couldn't tell me if the US Ambassador had reacted formally in defence of his man and would back-pedal once he had had time for consultation with Washington. And Paul wouldn't tell me what were the real intentions of the Canadian President. The Ambassador must have put considerable pressure on the old man, who would already have appreciated the self-evident fact that Coller's alleged communism had been exposed just too conveniently. I wondered what suspicions he had of me and Walter.

"You understand?" Paul said. "It's very difficult for us."

"I understand that while the Allies are quibbling among themselves this communist conspiracy is going to succeed," I said.

"That's very blunt, Mark. Off the record, I assume?"

"It was meant to be blunt, Paul, and not off the record. Anyway, I trust you'll keep me informed."

I nodded at him pleasantly and went to join Gaby, ignoring his half-spoken appeal. I did appreciate the Canadians' difficulties but I had too many problems of my own. The major one was the why and the where of John Coller's disappearance. But the first thing I had to do was to take my leave of Edgar and his family and get out of this hot, lily-scented room, so that I could go and take counsel with Nanny.

Woods-Dawson wasn't much help. The best he could do was advise masterly inaction. According to his assessment Coller was bound to turn up sooner or later, either innocently in Montreal or Ottawa or crying havoc in Washington. If the former he estimated that the President would seize his opportunity, jail Coller and declare to a grateful nation that he had saved them from the machinations of communism; subsequently the Americans would have no choice but to add their own condemnation of Coller. And we should have won.

But if Coller was in Washington, prepared to declare his innocence and give his own account of events, the Americans and the Canadians would procrastinate and the communists would take the initiative. They would immediately launch a campaign of violent protest against the British and the Americans and, at the same time, would cause the spurious Carmine document to be made public. It would then be too late for the President to take any action. And we should have lost, irretrievably.

Assuming that Woods-Dawson was right I had put our chances at evens. As the day lengthened, however, and there was still no news of Coller, I decided that the odds had turned against us. How I wished that I hadn't been quite so high-handed with Paul Brill. If the waiting had been bad before it was all but intolerable now, and I would have given almost anything to know what was going on and what efforts were being made to find Coller. But I had to contain my impatience—somehow.

Nor was I cheered when I got back from the Chancery and Gaby reminded me that we were dining with the Stockers. They were never my favourite hosts and tonight, with our relationship so strained, their hospitality couldn't have been less welcome. Unfortunately it was also unavoidable.

Gaby, Melanie and I arrived somewhat more than the conventional five minutes late, coinciding with another couple and Walter Eland. While we waited in the hall for the ladies to rejoin us I was able to have a word with Walter, who hadn't known that Coller's disappearance had caused an impasse.

He shook his head sadly. "I rather suspect, Mark, that both you and I are going to be looking for jobs soon. Do you think Melanie would help support me?"

"You'll have to ask her," I said.

"Ah well!" He shrugged away his bitterness. "I'll probably be manning the barricades anyway."

In the drawing-room there were already a dozen guests which meant that this was going to be an informal supper party in spite of the black tie invitation. Alex came forward to greet us, over-jovial and over-congratulatory about Walter's engagement to Melanie. There was no sign of Sally.

Then a tall, flat, narrow girl of about eighteen appeared. Alex introduced her as his daughter by his first marriage, who had come to spend a few months in Ottawa before going to university. We made polite conversation but she seemed extraordinarily nervous and eager to speak to Alex alone, so we left them together and joined the rest of the guests.

The hired help served drinks and the usual titbits. We drank and ate and chatted. It was a typical diplomatic party, pleasant or boring according to one's mood. Time passed. The noise level rose and then gradually subsided. People began to refuse drinks. One or two looked at their watches. But we couldn't go. We had been invited to dinner.

It must have been about now that I realized Sally still hadn't appeared. Alex's thin slab of a daughter was acting as hostess, drifting anxiously in and out of the room and trying to have whispered conversations with her father. I assumed that Alex and Sally had had a row and to spite him she intended to make a late entrance. Gaby, more charitable, suggested that she might be unwell. I didn't really care. I was hungry and out of humour.

I strolled over to Alex and said: "Are we waiting for Sally, Alex?"

It mayn't have been a tactful question but it didn't warrant the look he gave me, which was a mixture of hatred and frustration. Obviously there was nothing he would have liked better than to kick me in the teeth and, metaphorically speaking, this is precisely what he did.

He forced a tight smile and raised his voice. "I'm terribly sorry we're running late, everyone," he said. "But my wife, Sally, went on a shopping spree to Montreal this morning and she's not back yet. We shan't wait for her any longer, however. Let's go along to the dining-room."

There was a murmur of interest and commiseration. Somebody asked if Sally had gone by car and Alex said that she had but there was no need to worry because she was an excellent driver and the worst of the storm was over. She would be arriving any moment laden with parcels and apologies. He laughed at his own joke.

It didn't sound a very convincing laugh to me but nothing about his story was convincing. Yet it couldn't be a lie. If he had wanted to lie, I thought, he wouldn't have produced

such an extraordinary tale. Sally was impulsive; she might
well have decided on a day's shopping, even though Montreal
was still digging itself out from a fourteen-inch snowfall.
But it wasn't in character that she should have chosen this
particular day when they were giving a party for some twenty
people—not unless she had a very good reason indeed.

I couldn't believe it was coincidental that John Coller
had also gone to Montreal, and disappeared.

I managed to stand beside Gaby as we were all helping
ourselves at the buffet and whispered: "Try to find out from
the daughter what she knows about Sally going off to
Montreal, times, anything."

She looked at me in distress. "Oh Mark, it must be a
coincidence."

"You thought of it too?"

"Yes, but—" She swallowed. "All right. I'll try."

And later, when we were having coffee, she waylaid me.
"It was very easy," she said. "The girl's so angry at being
left to cope with the party. She says she heard someone
moving around about four this morning and thinks it was
Sally. Anyway, Sally had gone when the family got up and
there was a note on the breakfast table saying she was off
to Montreal for some shopping. Nothing about the party,
although they had been talking about it the night before,
and nothing about her small boy whom she was to take to
the dentist today."

"Hell!" I said, more loudly than I had intended.

"Something the matter, Mark?" Alex had overheard.

"No, nothing at all. We—er, we were just talking about
Sally," I said. "You must be worried that she hasn't even
telephoned?"

"Not really," he said, his face free of expression. "I
expect something delayed her and she decided to spend the
night with a friend of hers as she does sometimes. And the
line's out of order. I've tried it a couple of times."

"There're a lot of lines down round Montreal," Gaby
said. "The storm was even worse than here. Do Sally's
friends live right in the city?"

"They've a flat in Westmount, I believe." Alex was impatient. "I don't know them. Sally was at school with the

wife and they met again by chance. Can I get you some coffee, Gaby?"

"Please." She held out her cup to him.

He didn't bring it back himself but sent it by his daughter. Clearly he didn't want to discuss Sally any further and who could blame him? He must have been desperately worried, whatever he might say.

He can't have been more worried than I was, however. I was convinced by now that Alex had told Sally everything that I had told him not to and she had gone to Montreal to warn Coller. But why hadn't she come back? She might love the American enough to be prepared to leave Alex for him, if he would have her, but neither Gaby nor I believed that she would abandon her small son. This could only mean, as far as I could see, that she hadn't returned to Ottawa because she hadn't yet been able to locate and warn John Coller—unless, of course, she had had an accident.

I excused myself to the people who had been getting about a sixth of my attention, refused more coffee and made my way across the room to Melanie and Walter.

I said: "Listen. Alex has been telephoning Montreal. I must have the name and number—address, if possible." They both looked at me and gaped. "I've not the time to explain. Will one of you drift across the hall to the study. The telephone's there and one of those alphabetical pads that spring open. If he has been phoning at regular intervals he mightn't have shut it. It's an outside chance."

"Is this connected with—" Walter began and added, "I'll go."

I remembered then that I had never told him that Sally and Coller had been lovers; but this wasn't the moment for explanations. Either it was my guilty conscience or Alex was keeping an eye on me. I didn't want to make him suspicious of Walter too.

"Thanks," I said. "Be careful." I smiled and sauntered away.

For the next little while I tried to be an agreeable guest but it was difficult to concentrate on conversation which seemed to vary from the intense to the inane. Walter, I was glad to see, made no immediate move and when he did

Alex paid no attention to him. Although we had scarcely
finished the meal, Alex was busy offering everyone night-
caps. I suppose he wanted to get rid of us so that he could
devote himself to phoning Montreal.

He was doing his best to hide it but there was no doubt
he was upset and two or three of the more tactful guests
were leaving. Some of them, however, had forgotten about
Sally and looked prepared to make a night of it. I couldn't
help feeling sorry for the wretched Alex, at the same time
as I cursed him for his stupidity in confiding in Sally when
I had expressly told him not to. The idea of facing him with
the truth about her and demanding the address of the Montreal
apartment, where she and Coller might be, appalled me.
Moreover, I could easily imagine him calling me a liar and
refusing to co-operate.

I was glad when Walter came back into the room and
gave me a quick nod. I couldn't wait any longer and went
across to him.

"You were quite right," he said. "The pad beside the
phone was open—at the letter D. There were three English-
sounding names and Madame Marc Desberet." He spelled
it.

"Thank God for that," I said.

"I tried the number but the line's dead."

"Yes, Alex said it was. It could be the storm. Any address?"

"No, Mark, do you think he's there? Melanie told me
about his relationship with Sally Stocker. It would make
sense."

"He could be there or she mayn't have had the chance
to warn him yet. Anyway I propose to find out for myself.
Will you come with me?"

He didn't hesitate. "Of course. Try to stop me."

I grinned. "Thanks."

And we set off on what was to be a wild drive to Montreal.
The highway had been ploughed and there was little traffic,
but at the speed we were travelling the occasional patch of
black ice and blinding squall of blown snow made it a

hazardous journey. Twice we nearly came to a sticky end, once when the Rolls slid completely round and ended facing the wrong way in the wrong lane, and once when we mounted the verge and drove along it for some twenty yards. On the first occasion we were saved by the quick reactions of an oncoming driver and on the second by the skill of my chauffeur.

We reached the outskirts of Monteal about four a.m. and drove through the early-morning streets, empty except for the overworked snow-removal gangs, to the suburb of Westmount and the apartment of Monsieur and Madame Marc Desberet. We knew where we were going. Before leaving Ottawa I had telephoned Gavin Brown who had found the address by the simple means of looking in his local directory. The listing was under Desberet M. de C., whom I suspected of being one of John Coller's bachelor chums; I didn't expect to be confronted by an old school-friend of Sally's.

In the event, however, all my expectations were made to seem ridiculous.

The apartment block was small, and far from being luxurious. The glass door was locked but yielded quickly to a strip of plastic. There was no janitor or we never saw one. Presumably the occupants were not burglar-conscious.

We passed through the hall which even at this time of the morning smelt of Indonesian cooking and took the lift to the third floor. There were four flats on each floor. Desberet M. de C. occupied Number 33, overlooking the back of the building. While we waited to see if anyone would open the door, I wondered about fire-escapes. Nobody came. I put my finger on the bell and kept it there. Nothing happened. Nothing was going to happen. Neither John Coller nor Sally Stocker was here. I had guessed wrong.

And then I heard a sort of drumming noise. I pressed my ear against the door panel but the noise had stopped, if I hadn't imagined it. "Did you hear anything?"

Walter shook his head but my chauffeur, who had been inspecting the lock, said: "There's a light on inside, Sir Mark. You can see the hairline along the jamb."

We were all three close to the door, peering at the thread

of light, when the noise was repeated; and we all heard it.
This time it was more like a thumping, shuffling sound,
and it went on longer.

"What on earth do you think it is?"

"God knows. But I'm going to find out. Would you like
to wait for us, Walter? At the top of the stairs perhaps."

"And let you Brits get the credit for discovering Coller?
Most certainly not!"

It didn't take my chauffeur long to open the door; there
was a dead-lock but nobody had put it on—or the chain.
And we went in, straight into the living-room. The light
was on, as we had known it would be, and the first thing
we saw was Sally Stocker.

She was lying on the floor but still tightly bound to a
kitchen chair. She had a gag in her mouth, a choking gag
as I discovered when I tried to undo it. Her eyes were slightly
unfocused and full of hate. She had stopped rocking the
chair and pounding on the floor with her feet as soon as we
came into the room, but there were flecks of blood on wrists
and ankles where she had tried to burst her bonds. Around
her an overturned coffee table, a broken ashtray and other
signs of disorder showed that she hadn't given in easily.
Whatever her failings she didn't lack courage.

Our first impulse, Walter's and mine, was to free her.
My chauffeur was more practical. While Walter and I struggled to undo Sally he searched the flat. But he came back
carrying a glass of water for her.

"Nobody here, Sir Mark. And no back door or fire escape. The lady must have been alone."

The lady had drunk the water in great, noisy gulps and
was holding out her glass for more. Her breath came in
shallow but heavy gasps. Her skin, cold to the touch, was
beaded with sweat. Tears of anger and frustration had made
rivulets through her make-up. She looked dirty, exhausted
and afraid.

"She needs a doctor, Mark. The telephone."

"The telephone wire has been cut, sir."

"No. No doctor." Sally shook her head.

"See if you can find some brandy," I said to Walter.

"Oh Mark! Don't know why you came here but thank

God. Thank God! John said cleaning woman—in the morning—I didn't believe him. He told so many lies."

"John? John Coller did this to you, left you like this?" I was astounded.

"Yes."

"When? When did he go?" I demanded. "And how? What did he tell you? Sally, if we've the slightest chance of stopping him—"

"No—no chance. He caught a plane at ten—last night. He's there by now."

"So that's that," I said flatly, seeing my own despair mirrored in Walter's face. I had told him during the drive of Woods-Dawson's assessment, though leaving him blissfully unaware that I had set Coller up, and we had agreed that if Coller made for Washington and tried to brazen things out we were done. "God help us then!"

"Yes—and God damn John! Damn him! Damn him! The bloody communist!"

Sally had been fighting to control herself but now something snapped. She began to make extraordinary noises, half sobbing, half laughing, and whooping for breath. Hoping I was doing the right thing, I smacked her across the face; it was a stinging slap. There was dead silence. Then her eyes turned up and she passed out.

"God!" I was horrified.

"She'll be all right," Walter said at once. "Look, she's beginning to come round already. Let's put her on the sofa. And get some blankets from the bedroom, will you. She's shivering. It's shock, I suppose."

My chauffeur got the blankets and I watched Walter helping Sally to sit up and sip the brandy. My thoughts were racing. Nothing made sense. But it didn't really matter any more. Coller had gone. Sally had warned him and he had fled, incidentally gagging her and tying her to a chair. He was safe in the States now, crying—with justification—that someone was trying to make a scapegoat out of him. I hadn't any faith that the CFP would have picked him up at the airport; once he knew the danger he was in he would be clever enough to avoid it. He was, I remembered bitterly, one of CIA's top men and, the way things had turned out, they would do their best to protect him. Even if they failed, the complexities of the situation would cause a fatal delay.

Woods-Dawson's plan hadn't worked. The gambit hadn't paid off and subsequently the unfaceable consequences would have to be faced. In the meantime, *avant le déluge,* I could try to salvage some of the pieces.

I sent my chauffeur to telephone Gavin Brown that Mrs. Stocker would need a bed for a night or two and that we should all be glad of an early breakfast. Then I turned back to Sally. She was sitting up now, supported by Walter. There was colour in her cheeks and she looked reasonably normal. She also looked determined.

She said fiercely: "Alex didn't know anything about it, not anything at all. It was my fault. You can't blame him for my bloody-bloody stupidity." She almost spat the last words.

I pulled up a chair beside her—the kitchen chair to which she had been tied—and sat down. "If you're well enough," I said, "I'd like to know exactly what happened, from Monday evening when Alex came home and told you that John Coller was involved in a communist plot." I didn't really want to know but Woods-Dawson would demand details. "And the truth, Sally."

I could have spared her that. She had no inclination to lie at the moment, not even to save face, and I didn't doubt her when she said she hadn't believed Alex's story: she had thought that perhaps the Canadians were trying to frame Coller. Nevertheless, she had still hesitated about warning him. What had tipped the balance—and she couldn't appreciate the irony of this—was the news that Melanie was engaged to Walter. She had argued, with feminine logic, that the engagement proved her jealous suspicions of Melanie and Coller were unfounded, and therefore she owed it to John Coller to help him.

"Go on," I said, taking care not to look at Walter.

But Sally had broken down again and we had to wait. Walter fetched her some more brandy. I think he was glad of something to do. My chauffeur returned to say that Gavin Brown was expecting us. And, eventually, Sally resumed her predictable story.

At least it was predictable until, casually and in all innocence, she exploded what to me, who had never doubted Coller's integrity, was a bombshell.

John Coller had not gone to Washington; it seemed that was the last place he would have gone. Somebody had brought him an air ticket and a new passport—and he had caught the Moscow flight; it had been his good luck that Aeroflot had been delayed forty-eight hours because of the storm. John Coller was now in Russia. John Coller was, in fact, the communist agent which I had tried to make him appear.

And momentarily my world turned upside down.

EPILOGUE

"Next week the Minister for Power is to visit the Carmine Project with a team of experts. He will be accompanied by the British Ambassador, Sir Mark Lowrey. It is understood that Canada is to play a much more important role in the Project than presently."

The tough, aggressive features of the Minister were replaced on the television screen by a still of a squat building ornamented with odd protuberances and set in a vastness of ice and snow, an outward and visible sign of the Carmine Project as provided by the British Embassy. The announcer gave Carmine a splendid puff. Things had changed. Carmine was in; Carmine was Canadian—almost.

"So the Minister's to be accompanied by the British Ambassador. That puts you in your place, Mark."

"Which is precisely what the Minister intends. He has no love for the Brits and he's young and brash and slightly drunk with his own power."

"What you would call a right sod?"

"If I used such a phrase, Peregrine, yes. I certainly agree with the sentiment. I'm not looking forward to this trip to the Arctic with him."

"Too bad! You have my heartfelt sympathy, dear boy. Cheer yourself with the thought of what might have been."

I ignored Woods-Dawson's remark and got up to pour us both another whisky. The weather forecast had ended

194

and the newscaster reappeared, shuffling papers. As if bestowing a benison he informed us that there would now be some messages from our sponsors, which meant two minutes of advertisements seemingly aimed at morons. I didn't switch off the box; we were waiting for the President of Canada to address his people.

"My departure time for the frozen North is 0900 next Wednesday," I said without any emphasis.

Woods-Dawson laughed; he took the point. "I shall be leaving you on Sunday," he said, "if you'll arrange a first-class window seat on the BOAC flight for me."

"We've enjoyed having you," Gaby said, coming into the room and catching the end of our conversation. "Haven't we, Mark?"

"Yes, indeed," I said and meant it—not that I would be unhappy to see him go.

When Woods-Dawson had originally told me of his intention to come to stay with us I had been far from pleased, but I couldn't really object. It was understandable that he should want to discuss with me in person the events that had taken place over Christmas and the New Year, and the timing made it impossible for me to go to London. So my old school chum who just happened to be staying with cousins in Boston had flown up to Ottawa and, as it turned out, with Melanie back at Oxford and safely out of his way, the visit had been a success.

"You'll miss our farewell party for the Stockers, Peregrine."

"That pleases me, my dear Gaby."

"It would please us, too," I said, "but we have to go through the motions. *Diplomatie oblige.*"

And the Stockers were not our only obligation, I reminded myself with amused cynicism. We had suddenly had a spate of invitations to farewell parties as both the western and the eastern blocks of the Ottawa diplomatic corps reshuffled themselves after the outrage of John Coller's defection. It was inevitable, I suppose, just as the gossip was inevitable. At the moment Ottawa was riven with gossip connecting every likely and unlikely event with Coller. It was not, of course, pleasant, but Walter had been right when he said that as wilder and wilder stories flourished, rumours about Edgar's "accident" would lose all importance.

My musings were cut short by the man in the box. "And now the President of Canada," he declared.

Woods-Dawson bit off what he had been about to say, Gaby put down her drink untasted and we all leaned forward, intent upon the screen. For six seconds it was blank. Then there was the old man sitting regally behind an enormous desk. The camera panned in and we had a close-up of the heavy, tired face, dark and seamed, the melancholy eyes and the big, hooked nose—the face of a strong but devious man. For a minute he looked at us, gently, unsmiling; he didn't speak. He was a fine actor.

Then he said: "This evening I want to talk to you about the Carmine Project. No, don't turn off your sets and don't switch to an American channel! What I have to say is very important to you, to every Canadian. And don't worry." Suddenly he grinned showing his big white teeth. "I won't go on too long. I want to watch the hockey game too."

Alternating easily between French and English, the President explained the origins and purpose of Carmine and emphasized its importance to Canada. He said that many people had misunderstood the Project, that there had been false rumours linking it with the United States and a hate campaign against it had been whipped up by Canada's enemies with the express intention of embittering Canadians and turning them against their old friends.

"And the master-mind behind this plot to destroy the Carmine Project, to sow distrust between allies, to cause . . ."

The President ranted on for some minutes but I had stopped listening to him. Instead I was thinking about John Coller. I still found it difficult to believe that Coller was the communist agent that I had set him up to be. And it was even more difficult to accept that, if it had not been for my amateur efforts—not to mention Sally Stocker's—he would never have given himself away and thus brought the whole conspiracy to nothing.

I surfaced in time to hear the president say: ". . . grateful to Britain for her generosity." (So that there should be "no cause for any future misunderstanding" HMG was to cede fifty-one per cent interest in Carmine to Canada in return for an undisclosed sum; the money had been provided by the United States, or so Woods-Dawson had told me, adding that the President of Canada had played his cards well.) "And to Sir Mark Lowrey," the old man was continuing, "I am especially grateful—for his goodwill, his understanding and his co-operation during this trying time." He ended by giving his blessing to the people of Canada and all her friends.

"May they live in peace," Woods-Dawson said sardonically. He lifted his glass in my direction. "To you, dear boy. I too am grateful for the goodwill and co-operation of Sir Mark Lowrey." He grinned, and I wondered whether in the months to come my old chum, the Honourable Peregrine Woods-Dawson, or my new chum, His Excellency, the President of Canada, was likely to cause me most trouble. I drank to them both.

Don't miss...

A FAIR EXCHANGE

... Palma Harcourt's next gripping thriller,
coming in July.

*You'll want to read all of her books
published by Jove!*

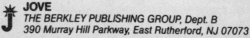